BONDED

BONDED

NEW EDEN BOOK 2

JESSICA MARTING

SHADOW PRESS

Bonded (New Eden Book 2)

ISBN 978-1-989780-34-3

Edited by Autumn Reed

Cover art by German Creative

Content notes: Discussion of a natural disaster and mass casualty event; discussion of intimate partner violence; parental death.

For David

INDIGNATION WARRED with excitement in Jasmine Sinclair as the hulking black starship shuddered, then began what felt like a wobbly ascent. With a squeal, she reached out for something to hold on to, grabbing a wall-mounted railing to regain her balance. She gazed out the small porthole at the field below them, then the ruins of New Eden's lone settlement as it came into view. The settlement became smaller as the ship rose in the air. A grinding sound rang in her ears, and she instinctively clapped her hands over them, letting go of the railing. She promptly fell against the porthole. "Damn!"

Strong hands helped her upright. A shiver raced through her, and she turned around to see SP29—cyborg with a green thumb, her housemate, and her reason for her indignation in the first place. "You should strap in. The heavy air engine has a hell of a kick," he said over the noise.

Where was she supposed to strap in? She looked around the ship's lounge, then let out an exasperated sigh as she took in the distinct lack of jump seats. Instead, she resumed her grip on the railing. Her reaction actually drew a smile from him, and her heart, stupid thing it was, did an equally stupid flip-flop against her ribs.

Why the hell was she still attracted to him? Why the hell did he have to be so hot? Not only that, how could someone that hot be so hot and cold toward her? If nothing else, Jasmine was determined to wheedle his reasons for shutting her out on this, her first voyage into space. Before he'd cut himself off from her, he'd promised to take her off New Eden, regaling her with stories about other planets and waystations. She was determined to hold him to that promise.

"How long does this last?" she asked him over the heavy air engine's roar. If space travel was this loud, she would need to invest in something to use as earplugs, stat.

SP29 looked like he was counting off the seconds. She watched him mouth the numbers until he reached zero, then . . . silence. As the ship gave a final shudder, the view outside changed to black. The deck stilled, vibrations ceasing. A hum briefly filled the air, and with it, Jasmine's stomach turned over. She let go of the railing and fell back against the wall, fighting a wave of nausea.

"The grav function has just stabilized," SP29 announced, answering her question before she could ask it. He helped her up again. As if he just remembered who he was dealing with, his expression shuttered. "I'll show you to your quarters."

Jasmine thought about the rows of recharging pods that lined the ship's corridors. "I can't sleep upright."

It was meant to be a lighthearted quip, and if this was back in the cyborgs' early days on New Eden, it would have coaxed a smile from him. Instead, his expression remained stormy. His eyes glowed red for a few seconds, a sure sign that he was processing their situation. "I know that. We lived together."

They still did, technically. SP29 had moved into Jasmine's living room in her ramshackle house when the cyborgs arrived on New Eden. She tried not to smart over the word "lived," as if he intended to move out as soon as they returned home. "All right," she said, voice small. She picked up her tattered feed sack, crammed with things she thought she might need on an interstellar voyage. It had fallen over during the ship's launch, her two changes of clothes spilling onto the deck. She shoved them back inside and followed him through the ship.

Thus far, Jasmine had only seen the cockpit, lounge, sickbay, and recharging pods. SP29 led her through a corridor that reeked of disuse. Unlike the parts of the ship she'd seen so far, with their bare metal decks and walls, this area was carpeted, the fibers plush under her sandaled feet. The walls were painted a calming blue, affixed with an occasional art piece every few meters. She blinked in surprise. "Where did these paintings come from?"

"Previous iterations and things we picked up over the years," SP29 replied.

"Did you do them, or one of your previous clones?"

"No. The original Samuel didn't have an artistic bone in his body, and neither do I."

He rarely spoke about what he called his *original*, the human organic from which he and his previous twenty-eight clones descended from. Or was it twenty-nine? Did they count the first clone? Jasmine thought it might be rude to ask.

SP29 stopped outside the first door they reached and pressed a button next to it. It slid open with a slight hiss. "Home sweet home."

She put aside her irritation to walk over the door's

tread. Though the room was spare, it housed the biggest bed she'd ever seen, made up with steel-gray covers that looked new. A table and pair of chairs were bolted to the deck, beside a giant window that offered a stunning view of open space. A bathroom was visible to her left, its tiles blindingly white. Yet another oil painting was arranged on the wall, this one a sweeping landscape of a field filled with blue-tipped grass, a brilliant pink sun overhead. "Where's that?" she asked excitedly, pointing to it.

"I don't know. I think one of DL16's previous clones may have painted that, but I'm not sure."

"You mean Darius?"

Something unreadable flashed in SP29's eyes. Pain, maybe? "Yes," he replied evenly.

Maybe it was the nausea that still roiled around in Jasmine's stomach since the ship took off, or maybe it was their forced proximity looming ahead of them over the next few days that caused her irritation to boil over. "SP29, what's going on?"

He shrugged, a very human response. Of course it would be, she reminded herself. He was mostly human, with a couple of metal parts. Was one of those metal parts his heart? "What's going on?" she repeated.

"What do you mean?"

"You know," she said. "Everything was fine between us on New Eden until a couple of days ago. You promised I could go with you off-world and told me all about the places you'd show me. And now you're acting like you don't want to know me at all, like I'm a giant inconvenience to you." Tears threatened behind her eyes, but she willed them away. "Did I say something wrong?"

His expression finally softened. "No."

"Then, tell me why you're acting weird."

"We're cyborgs. We're all a little weird."

"You aren't! You've been one of the most human cyborgs I've met." She thought about Rhys, their de facto leader and now her best friend Hannah's boyfriend. Rhys had been one of the stiffest, most socially awkward people Jasmine ever met. He'd been the living stereotype of a cyborg, at least the ones she'd read about in old novels brought to New Eden by the original settlers. "I thought we were friends," she continued, voice small. She'd had so few. Living in a dying settlement as she was, her family dead, Hannah closed off from everyone in her grief since a disastrous earthquake struck their planet.

SP29 scrubbed a hand over his face. "We are," he said, voice halting. "Look, hurting your feelings wasn't my intention. This is a very complicated situation for me, and I'm not sure how to handle it."

"What's complicated? I thought we liked each other." There. That was now out in the open. They'd flirted and joked together almost as soon as he moved into her living room, and she'd been sure they would be a couple at some point. His abrupt, cold rejection had hurt her more than she ever expected.

"I do," he said. "Like you, I mean. There are other factors at play here." His closed expression returned, as if he'd said too much.

"What other factors?" When he didn't immediately respond, she continued pushing him for answers. "Cyborg things? Are you talking about Rhys? Because you fixed him."

He hesitated before replying. "Of a sort. I don't think emergency brain surgery would repair what's going on with me."

Alarm threaded through her. "Are you dying? Are you

going to be cloned again?" Now she truly understood Hannah's panic when Rhys had his surgery after his collapse. A new RH104—or whatever number he would be—would not be the same person she'd fallen in love with. Jasmine was attracted to SP29. She didn't want to entertain thoughts about an SP30.

"No, I'm not dying. Nothing's breaking down." She leaned forward, hoping he would tell her more. "I'm going to need some time to think about this," he finally said.

"How much time?"

"I don't know."

"Are you mad at me?"

To her surprise, he gave her a smile tinged with sadness. "No. The opposite, in fact." He tilted his head to the side, a surefire sign that someone on the shared cyborg broadcast link was talking to him. "We'll talk later, okay? Get settled in here."

Jasmine looked around the space. There wasn't much to settle in to, but she recognized a dismissal when she heard it. "All right. I'll hold you to that."

———

SP29 STALKED THROUGH THE SHIP, back to the sections he felt most comfortable in. Carpet gave way to metal on the deck, the dull thud of his boots against it satisfying. He wanted to go back to Jasmine's quarters and tell her everything, but couldn't. Nor could he speak to Darius yet, much as he needed to.

No one had spoken to him on the broadcast comm, but he needed to get away from her. Needed to clear his head. That was the whole point of leaving her and Darius behind on New Eden, but both of them had ended up aboard the ship, to his consternation. Darius had wanted to hit up the nearest waystation for frivolous things: holos, newsdisks, and food lacking any kind of nutritional value, in addition to the supplies New Eden so desperately needed. As for Jasmine . . . he'd promised to take her along the first time the ship left, a vow he now regretted. One he would have easily been able to break if she was a heavier sleeper, someone who could slumber through a starship's engines revving to life.

There were two days to fill until they reached the nearest waystation. Two days of being stuck on a ship with a skeleton crew, two of whom were people he was pretty sure he was in love with. More than that, he suspected they had feelings for him as well. SP29 was better at reading unenhanced human body language than most of his cyborg brethren. He could tell when someone was attracted to him, as Jasmine was. As was Darius, and they'd acted on their mutual attraction before they'd arrived on New Eden.

The bridge door read his bioprint and automatically opened for him. It was empty, as he'd expected, the ship running on an automatic course. He collapsed into the captain's seat and leaned back, staring up at the ceiling's embedded lights. "The hell am I supposed to do?" he mumbled. To distract himself, he ran down a mental checklist of the things he was supposed to procure at the waystation. Comms equipment, building materials, a hard goods replicator that could be bastardized to work with New Eden's unique electricity generator . . .

The bridge door opened. SP29 didn't have to turn his head to know who the interloper was. "Not now."

Darius slid into the copilot's seat next to him and splayed out, mimicking his position. "Why not?"

SP29 closed his eyes. "Because I don't want to."

"You've cut yourself off from everyone on the link."

He shrugged. "I don't feel like having everyone in my head." For a moment, the only sound in the bridge was Darius's breathing.

Any hopes of quiet contemplation evaporated when Darius said quietly, "I miss you."

SP29 sidestepped that admission, even though the words pulled at his heart in a way that had nothing to do with his cybernetics being faulty. "How busy has the link been, anyway? It seems like everyone's integrating with the New Edeners and prefers to communicate the old-fashioned way." He thought back to his last conversation on the link with Rhys. A middle of the night chat where he'd confessed his feelings for Darius and Jasmine. Rhys, to his everlasting credit, didn't offer the advice that SP29 hadn't been searching for. Instead, Rhys had merely listened to him. He'd needed that judgment-free support. He still did.

Darius shifted, based on the sound his clothes made against the hard material on the thin seat cushions. "I need to talk to you," he said urgently, voice low, as if he was afraid someone would barge in on them.

Damn it, SP29 needed to talk to him, too, but hadn't found the right words yet. It was on the tip of his tongue to argue, but what came out instead was, "I know. I need to talk to you too." He sighed.

"Is it about the last night on the waystation or Jasmine?"

SP29 felt himself blanch. "Why are you so fucking perceptive?"

"It comes with the territory when your original was some kind of psychologist. I can read people well. I also know you better than anyone else."

SP29 finally looked at him. Darius's expression was one

he recognized well, open and full of longing. He missed SP29 just as much as SP29 missed him. Part of him wanted to break down, tell him how discombobulated he was, how adrift he felt. Untethered. But the words wouldn't come yet. All he could do was lie and say, "You don't." And without another word, he left the bridge.

CHAPTER TWO

He wasn't coming back.

Jasmine couldn't help but feel rejected at SP29's abrupt about-face. She had thrown herself onto the bed while the ship shuddered along, breathing deeply against the nausea. She wasn't sure how much time passed before she finally crawled to her feet, anxious to get her sea legs. Or space legs, she supposed. She had never been in a boat, either, but she had read about them and spaceships in books years ago. Back when New Eden had a library in its community center, but of course, that was a pile of rubble now. Even before the earthquake that changed New Eden forever, the books had been old and falling apart. There had been no way to get new ones after the planet's sole printing press had been dismantled for parts when she was four or five years old.

The cabin door opened automatically for her, a novelty. She stepped over the door tread a couple of times, marveling at the tech that had to be old hat for everyone else in the civilized universe, until she remembered why she'd forced herself off the bed. "Exploration," she muttered under her breath. When would she get a chance to do so again?

She retraced her steps back to the spare, cold corridor that she was familiar with, and made a mental note to ask someone about the decorated part of the ship. What it had once been used for. She passed a couple of open doors, the machines inside unfamiliar to her, and two cyborgs whose designations she couldn't remember nodded their heads at her as she passed. At least her presence wasn't bothering them.

"Where is he?" she murmured.

"Please repeat your question." The voice came out of nowhere.

Jasmine shrieked. "Who the fuck was that?"

"This is the ship's AI." The answer was male, brusque, and matter-of-fact.

As Jasmine's heart returned to a normal speed, she mulled over that new bit of information. She had only ever read about artificial intelligence in books. New Eden's founders had fled the old world and all of its comforts for a low-tech excuse for an existence. Excitement grew in her at the possibility of speaking to a computer that could reply in kind. "Really?"

The reply was automatic. "Yes."

"Oh, wow."

"I am not programmed to respond to that. Please rephrase your question."

"Oh, it's not a question."

"Please rephrase your—"

"Yeah, I get it. Uh, where would I find SP29?"

"The clone designated SP29 has retired to his charging pod."

So, he was napping, then. And he loved his sleep as much as she loved hers, she recalled. "What about

Darius?" He was the only other cyborg aboard that she knew fairly well. Her heart skipped a couple of beats when she thought of him, the sensation as intense as it was when she looked at SP29.

It's probably because they're the only men I've spoken to in years. She and her body were reacting to the novelty of being around them. If she'd grown up in a normal society, she wouldn't be contemplating what it would be like to have two boyfriends, instead of one.

"Please specify the clone designation."

"Damn it. Uh, D something?" He'd had a lower numerical designation assigned to his initials, indicating he hadn't been cloned as often as the others. "Sixteen, that's it!"

"DL16 is in the lounge."

"Awesome." At least he was in a spot she could find.

The AI didn't offer a rejoinder, which was a little disappointing. She would have liked to have had a conversation with it, to see how close its conversation skills were to that of real people. Maybe it was incapable of colloquial chitchat.

True to the AI's word, she found Darius in the lounge, dark eyes gone silver as he downloaded something in his head. She'd seen that happen to a couple of cyborgs. Though startling at first, the sight didn't bother her anymore.

Seeing Jasmine in the doorway, the furrow between his brows smoothed out, and a smile spread across his face. His eyes changed back to normal. "Hey."

"Am I interrupting anything?"

"No, I'm just watching a serial. I downloaded a couple of new episodes after we broke atmosphere. How are you finding space travel?"

Jasmine didn't realize she was holding on to the

doorway until he asked. She'd been too distracted by how he looked when he smiled. "I thought the gravity function might be better."

Darius laughed. "Seriously?" Just as quickly, his mirth evaporated. "Sorry, that was rude. I know you're from a low-tech planet."

"No offense taken. And I think New Eden qualifies as a no-tech planet."

"Come on, your people harnessed hydroelectric power."

"Which society hasn't?" Jasmine sank into the deck-locked chair opposite Darius's. "Anyway, my point is, I thought the gravity function on a ship like this would be better. I don't know how to describe how I feel right now."

"Try."

Darius pinned her with a stare that made her want to squirm in her seat. Not for the first time, she wondered if he would look at her like that in bed. Jasmine considered her words, still uncertain of how to describe how it felt to be in space. "This is how I imagine being seasick might feel like. I've never been on a boat, so I can't be sure."

"You'd probably be losing your lunch all over the deck if the seasickness was that bad," Darius pointed out.

"I thought I might for a bit when SP29 first showed me to my cabin."

Something shifted in his expression at the mention of SP29's name. Just as quickly, it was gone, and Darius was back to his jovial self.

Interesting. Jasmine had never picked up on any kind of animosity between the cyborgs. They were more tightly knit than most of the New Edeners, who had been at one another's throats for years.

"How do you like the accommodations?" Darius asked, changing the subject.

"They're really nice. It's like something out of a book," Jasmine replied enthusiastically. "Why's that part of the ship so pretty?"

"Those cabins were built for guests. Our previous clones didn't see the point in wasting the resources to convert the cabins to recharging pods, so they were left as is."

"I thought you built this ship?" Jasmine asked, intrigued.

"We acquired it and modified it to our needs. Our previous clones did, at least," he added.

Not for the first time, Jasmine wondered how many memories each one cyborg had from previous bodies. Rhys had been plagued by memories and flashbacks, although he'd been cloned dozens of times. SP29 and Darius hadn't been replicated nearly as much. That had to have something to do with their being less stiff and formal, more comfortable with unenhanced humans, than Rhys was.

"Well, I love the cabin," Jasmine reiterated. "And I'm sure I'll get used to the space sickness or it'll go away soon."

"We have meds that'll take care of that."

She perked up. She should have expected that, but she was so used to doing without that it hadn't occurred to her to ask. "You do?"

Darius rose and crossed the room, standing in front of a black, glass-fronted cabinet. He touched it and it lit up. A comp screen. Jasmine followed him, fascinated, her nausea temporarily forgotten. Darius flicked the screen with his fingers until a grid appeared on it, each box marked with a different letter and number. He selected one, tapping his fingertip against it twice. A low grinding noise sounded, then a square in the screen slid open to reveal a compartment, a small, flat, blue paper rectangle lying inside.

Darius picked it up between two fingers. "Hold out your arm."

There was an authoritative note to his voice that sent a shiver through her spine that had nothing to do with the ship's temperature. She did as she was told.

Darius rubbed the patch against her skin until it stayed in place. Heat traveled up her skin at the contact. She felt herself flush. She hoped he didn't notice.

"Everything okay?" he asked.

She nodded. "Yes, thank you. What will this do?" She peered at the rectangle. To her surprise, it melted into her skin, the blue color getting lighter until it disappeared.

"It'll help with your motion sickness until you've acclimated to the ship. We should get you vaccinated before we hit the waystation, too, unless . . ." He stopped himself. "Fuck it. You wouldn't have had anything like that."

"No."

He tilted his head, studying her. "Are you sure you're all right? My hardware is telling me that your heart rate is up a bit and your temperature rose by a quarter of a degree."

Goddamn it all. At the realization that he knew the effect he was having on her, she pushed away any lascivious thoughts. "I'm totally fine." She pasted a smile on her face and held up her arm. "See? I'm not barfing." Turning to the now-darkened comp screen, she changed the subject. "Do you need to take the nausea meds?"

"No, our programming takes care of that."

She felt like an idiot. Of course, it would. "What about the vaccinations you talked about? I don't want to bring anything back to New Eden."

"Working on that now." With inhuman speed, Darius's fingers tapped the comp until the receptacle box opened below the screen with a near-silent hiss. Another square of paper appeared, this one green. Darius pressed it against her forearm, his touch warm and firm. Jasmine tried not to shiver, even as goose bumps popped up along her skin. "That should keep you healthy while we're at the waystation."

He didn't let go of her immediately. Indecision warred on his features before he removed his hand. Jasmine immediately missed the contact but had no idea how to initiate it again. She nodded at the comp. "What else does that thing do?"

It worked. Darius shifted his attention away from her physical reaction to him and showed her how to use the comp screen. A replicator, he called it, just like the tech Jasmine had read about. It was programmed to dispense basic medicine and dehydrated food cubes, none of which looked especially appealing but would keep her fed while aboard the ship. "Of course, we can always pick up some treats for you on the waystation." His dark eyes sparkled with promise.

Damn it, there was that fluttery, hot feeling again. "I'd like that."

His gaze searched hers. "Are you sure you're okay? Your temperature rose again just now."

She nodded. "I'm fine."

This was going to be an even longer voyage than she'd expected.

———

HE WAS BEING RUDE. An utter asshole.

SP29 stalked the length of the ship's gym, ignoring the equipment. Part of him ached to beat the shit out of the punching bag in the corner, designed precisely for that purpose; it had even been reinforced to handle cybernetic strength. He didn't want to, knowing that if he gave in, he wouldn't stop until the thing was nothing more than a pile of stuffing and synthetic leather. He knew he wasn't acting like himself and that he owed Darius and Jasmine apologies.

Unfortunately, he didn't have a lot of experience with apologizing. It wasn't that he wasn't willing to do it. He went out of his way to be amiable and considerate to others, so he wouldn't have to be in a position to apologize.

He gritted his teeth as another, unrelated subject forced its way to his mind's forefront. He needed a name. His previous iterations had had a few over the years, with his original being called Samuel. He didn't see the point in changing his initials, and reverting to his original's name didn't hold much appeal. "Simon," he muttered under his breath. That would do. He liked its simplicity. More than that, he didn't want to be Samuel again. The original Samuel had been up to some shady shit.

He eyed the punching bag. Why the fuck shouldn't he punch it? He slammed into it with a fierce right hook.

He knew what Samuel Pelletier had done in another lifetime, two centuries ago, by the estimation of the other cyborgs. Knew it and was disgusted with it, even though he had tried to set things right later. But he knew now that there was no undoing what the original cyborg and cloning program had set into motion.

"SP29?"

The sound of Jasmine's voice in the doorway pulled him out of his musings, and he straightened. Instinctively, he ran his fingers through his short hair, hoping he didn't look too deranged.

She cautiously stepped into the gym and took in the space, eyes wide. "Is this where you've been hiding?"

He nodded.

"So, you admit you were hiding?" She put her hand on her hip, eyeing him suspiciously in a way she probably meant to look authoritative. With her long, white-blond hair hanging in her bedroom eyes, the effect was more seductive. It was easy to imagine her doing the same pose in something black and lacy, framed by a bedroom doorway.

He took a deep breath, willing away salacious thoughts of her.

Instead, he zeroed in on the small blue medical patch on her arm and idly wondered where she got it. He nearly asked on the link he shared with the other cyborgs but stopped himself in time. He hadn't been a part of it for a while and wasn't ready to have the others in his head again.

She was waiting for an answer. "I have," he said. May as well be honest.

"Why?"

"I've decided to call myself Simon from now on." He hadn't meant to say that.

She raised a pale eyebrow in approval. "I like *Simon*. And you're not answering my question."

"I'm not good at this," he said bluntly.

She lifted her shoulders in a shrug, her expression aghast. "And? Did you think I'd hold that against you? I'm not good at this, either!"

"You're human."

"So are you! Just with an electric heart and pancreas."

He could see what she was trying to do—pick up where they left off before he started struggling with his feelings. He wished he could return her banter. He'd found he could do that so easily with her.

And with Darius. They were the only two people he'd ever really loosened up around.

She took a few steps closer to him and poked him in the chest. "Even an electric heart is still a heart," she said. The hurt in her voice pulled at him. This close, he could smell the faint scent of her homemade soap, overlaid with a lemony fragrance from the herbs native to New Eden. For half a second, he wondered if her parents had named her after the old world flower.

"It isn't electric," was all he could say. "Hearts function on electrical impulses. Mine has been cybernetically enhanced, but . . ."

"You know what I mean." Her dark blue eyes fixed on him, pinning him with a hard stare.

"Yes."

"So, why have you been acting like this? I thought things were going great between us. You promised I could come with you to the waystation, and then you nearly left without me. What the hell is that? And don't tell me you need time to think."

"It's the truth."

She'd removed her finger, but she remained rooted in place on the deck, glaring at him as she waited for an explanation.

"My feelings for you are complex," he finally said.

The answer only slightly mollified her. "In what way?" She took a shaky breath. Her voice was tinged with hurt. "I like you. I thought you liked me too."

"I do."

"Then, why are you being so fucking weird? And don't give me that 'it's complicated' bullshit. You don't think my living through an ecological temper tantrum isn't complicated?"

Guilt twanged through him when he thought about the earthquake that had ravaged New Eden. It was the whole reason his people and hers made contact in the first place.

All the surviving New Edeners had experienced tremendous loss even before the quake.

She deserved the truth. "I had a breakup recently." Was "breakup" the right word for two people who had no idea how to maintain a relationship after a couple of nights together on a waystation while the ship was being refueled?

She stared at him, agog. "How? I thought you guys just cruised through space, minding your own business."

"We do." He didn't elaborate, unsure how to.

Jasmine didn't push for more details, which he was grateful for. "I wish you'd told me. I'm a little more understanding than that." She looked away, but not before Simon saw tears film over her eyes.

Oh, hell.

"Hey," he said quietly. Her blue gaze caught his, unshed tears still there. "I'm glad I told you. It's hard for me to get back into relationships when the last one ended so badly." He steeled himself, bracing for his next words. "It was the first one for both of us. We weren't good at it."

"You had a very different experience, compared to Rhys."

He wondered what Hannah had told her about Rhys. Their de facto leader was quiet, reserved, had all but programmed away his own emotions before he met Hannah. "I did. Look, I care about you very much. I'm just incredibly bad at this."

"Did you think I'd do any better? Did you notice the dearth of eligible men on New Eden?"

That was a good point. "Yes."

"Okay, so we're both bad and inexperienced at this. If you decide you want to be terrible at this together, you know where my cabin is."

It was the nicest one on the ship, a deliberate choice on his part. "Yeah."

"You also know where I live on New Eden."

"Well, yeah. I've been crashing on your couch for weeks." Something in him unfurled itself and relaxed. Banter with her, he could do. He could handle this.

"So, when you're ready, you know where to find me." She turned around and was about to walk out of the gym, but on impulse, Simon grabbed her hand.

"Wait," he said.

She turned huge eyes to him, lips parted. Before he could talk himself out of it, he kissed her. She froze, and for a heart-stopping half second, he thought he'd made a horrible mistake.

Then she responded, tongue at his lips, demanding entrance. He was only too happy to offer it, tangling his with hers. His heart stuttered in a way that could only happen to a human before his arms locked around her waist, bringing her closer to him. She gave a little mewl of surprise as he lifted her a few centimeters off the deck, then reached for his jaw, fingertips tracing along his skin. His own temperature rose, blood rushing so quickly through his veins that he thought she might actually be able to hear it. His cock immediately swelled. He instinctively reached for the hem of her T-shirt, then stopped as soon as his fingers touched her skin. If he didn't stop now, he would do something reckless and make everything worse.

Reluctantly, he pulled away. She looked up at him with half-lidded eyes, lips swollen. "Wow," she murmured.

He felt the same way. He was at a loss for words, not wanting to spoil what had just happened between them.

"Does this mean you're going to stop being weird and distant?" she asked. "I can't deal with any more head games."

He smiled. "I'll try my best not to be weird and distant."

She placed her hand over his heart and stilled. "I can't feel anything unusual."

He lifted an eyebrow. "It's working, I assure you."

"But is it going into overdrive like mine is?"

He could sense that, just as his own enhancements told him his heart was beating faster than usual. "Yes."

She dropped her hand. "Good."

Simon felt like a giant knot of tension had been unwound. There was the other knot to deal with—Darius was aboard the ship too—but at least Jasmine didn't hate him. "I'm glad we had this talk."

"Come by my cabin if you want to do more than that." A thrill shot through him at the suggestion. She quickly added, "Wow, I did *not* expect to hear myself say that today."

"I may take you up on that, but I'm not sure it'll be aboard the ship."

"Good." She gave him a saucy smile, then turned her face up to his for another kiss. "I mean, 'good that you want to visit me that way,' not 'good, don't come to my cabin, anyway.' I'm going to explore a little before I do something stupid."

At least she was on the same page as him. "I'm sure we'll run into each other later."

She was already at the doorway. Over her shoulder, she said, "I'll see you later, Simon."

He liked how his new name sounded coming from her. More real, more human.

CHAPTER THREE

Darius had little need for rest. Whether that was a quirk he'd inherited from his original and iterations over the years, or something programmed into his cybernetics, he couldn't say. He regarded it as a feature, not a bug, even on the ship's designated recharging hours. He slowly wandered the darkened ship while everyone else was resting, lost in thought.

There had been something *different* about Simon. It wasn't just that he'd finally decided on a name for himself. Darius didn't need his sensors to know that Simon's emotions had been running high after . . . well, whatever had happened. Jasmine had remained tightlipped about it, too, but Darius still noticed the secret looks they'd exchanged throughout the evening meal of rehydrated rations. Jealousy flared through him, and he didn't know who or what he was most envious of: that Simon and Jasmine's fragile relationship was on the mend, or that he wasn't involved with either.

Or both. He'd entertained more than a few fantasies about having both of them in his bed. As he strode the ship's corridors, lights shut off in a bid to conserve fuel, he smiled to himself while thinking about Jasmine between him and Simon. His night vision guided him as he padded along the bare decks in sock feet. He welcomed the light thrum of the engine under him, a little thing about space travel that he had missed during his time on New Eden.

Although, when he thought of New Eden, he thought about the planet's twin suns and abundant vegetation. He'd never known a place so green and fresh before. Now that he was back aboard the ship, he found himself missing the planet.

The sensor array in his brain kept him connected to the ship, similar to the way he communicated with his brethren. He could feel everyone asleep in their recharging pods, and he wondered if they missed their proper beds on New Eden. He could sense Jasmine's cabin too, now that its functions were online. She'd turned up its heat controls before she went to bed. Guilt thrummed through him at his not considering her lack of experience with the cold. Ships were chilly in deep space, and the cyborgs could regulate their temperatures at will. Jasmine didn't own so much as a heavy sweater. New Eden vacillated from warm and rainy in its short winters to unbearably hot in its extended summer season. He and the rest of the cyborgs had arrived in early summer, while it was comfortably hot. He'd enjoyed the feeling of sunlight on his face. All of them had.

He stopped by the lounge and ordered water from the dispenser. Sliding into a hard-backed chair, he tripped the code in his occipital lobe's sensor. He'd downloaded a few popular broadcasts into it, and he activated a program. A frothy, fluffy comedy that was produced by an entertainment conglomerate on 4-Colter-X, it was something Rhys had heavily disapproved of when he was still RH103.

Darius had dozens of them saved from when they still lived on their destroyed terraformed asteroid.

Acknowledging New Eden's distress signal and ordering the ship to set a course for the small planet had done all of them some good, especially Rhys. The most-cloned cyborg of all of them, he'd had a rod up his ass until they made contact with the New Edeners and struck a deal with them for shelter in exchange for new infrastructure.

The broadcast filled his vision, replacing the dark lounge, as he settled into his chair. He had watched it a couple of times already, a twenty-minute episode of a serial about a pair of inept Voralian petty criminals. He had been looking forward to downloading the rest of the series when this supply run had first been announced.

Something rustled in the back of his mind, interrupting his viewing. The serial's image cleared and his normal vision returned. His eyes automatically adjusted to night vision.

It was someone in the recharging pods, waking up. Darius didn't have to check the cyborg's ident chip to know it was Simon. He didn't get up, knowing Simon would likely wander the ship until he found Darius in the lounge.

He was correct. A few moments later, he wandered in, eyes glowing green. Despite having slept upright, cyborg style, he'd forgone his old flight suit that kept him connected to the ship in favor of a pair of old trousers. Darius's pulse quickened at the side of his bare upper half. "I thought I'd find you here," Simon said sleepily, then yawned.

"Where else would I be?"

"Maybe you wanted to watch your cartoons on the bridge, I don't know."

"No need for me to be there with the course we've plotted." Darius disliked bridge duty. He had a vague memory from his original, or a previous iteration, of a cockpit fire and suspected that was where the aversion came from. He hadn't looked into it too much. Darius preferred to live in the present. "Besides, I'd know if something went wrong," he added.

"Look, I'm glad I ran into you." Simon blinked his glowing eyes. "Would you mind if I switched on the lights?"

Darius's breath quickened. Did Simon want to see him as much as he wanted to see Simon? "Of course not."

The illumination panels inset a few centimeters off the floor switched on, giving off a pale yellow glow. Simon unclipped a chair from its deck lock and moved it closer to Darius's, then sat again. His dark hair stuck up at odd angles, and there was a faint trace of beard along his jaw. Darius grinned at the sight. Evidently, Simon had decided to allow that bodily process to resume since their arrival on New Eden. Something in his expression must have given away his notice, because Simon said, "What?"

"I like the scruff."

A few hours ago, that reply would have put a sour look on Simon's face. Now, he only smiled. Darius had missed that. "I'm feeling more human than machine these days. I may as well look the part."

"Why not take a cabin with a bed?"

"I miss the rest of you too much to do that." He grinned. Just as quickly, the expression faded. "Look, I have to tell you something."

"Are you breaking up with me for real this time?" Despite his flippant words, Darius's insides squeezed painfully.

"I'm not sure we were ever together, but—" Simon

shook his head. "I'm not opening that can of worms again."

"I resent being considered a 'can of worms.'"

Simon looked suitably chastised at his reply. "You're right. You're not. That came out badly. We never really had a label for what we are . . ."

Darius brightened at the use of the present tense.

"Just that it's a complex situation. I don't want to wreck the dynamics of the crew if we were open about us." Simon sighed. "Anyway, the point I'm trying to get to is that I kissed Jasmine today."

Darius had suspected something had occurred between them. Once again, jealousy reared its ugly head in him. "In the gym?"

"How did you know we were there? Were you keeping tabs on us?"

Darius gave him his best withering look. "Sensors, and of course, I kept tabs on you." He didn't try to hide the hurt in his voice, despite the flippancy in his next words. "So, have you chosen Jasmine over me?"

Simon hesitated. Darius's heart sank, sending flares of hurt through his chest. He tried to keep his expression neutral, not wanting to give away his pain at being rejected. "I haven't *chosen* Jasmine like that," he said quietly. "I'm glad we cleared the air, and I came here because I want to do the same with you."

"So you can better decide who you want to be with?" He nearly blurted out that Simon could have both of them if he wanted, that he was amenable to sharing and more than a little intrigued by the notion. His hurt was replaced by excitement over the possibility of the three of them being together.

"No. I don't want to have to choose."

The admission surprised Darius. Possibilities ran through his mind. "Maybe you don't have to."

Simon froze, green eyes fixed on his. Darius's own breath caught. He didn't dare move, not wanting to startle Simon. He knew, if he did, Simon would get up and stalk back to the recharging pods, and Darius would still be feeling lonely and confused.

Finally, Simon said, "I wish it was that simple. In what universe would it be easier to be in a relationship with two people instead of one?"

"Mine, I guess," Darius replied.

A smile played across Simon's face. Darius wanted to kiss it. "Not mine, and I'm not sure it would be in Jasmine's, either. We also have to think of the New Edeners. I don't know if that sort of arrangement would be well-received there."

Darius stared at him. "Who cares? I highly doubt the New Edeners would, when their concerns are likely to be about building a hospital. We're all adults." He leaned forward, resting his elbows on his knees. "What are you so terrified of?"

"I'm bad at this."

"So am I. Did you really expect a secluded group of traveling cyborg clones, or an even more secluded dying colony, to be good at relationships? We weren't cloned knowing those things."

Simon glared at him, all traces of his smile gone. It pained Darius. He wanted to see it again, wanted to be the cause of it. "I just don't know," he muttered.

"You have time to think about it. You know Jasmine and I will always listen to you." He fumbled over her name. It would hurt more than he could imagine if Simon chose her over him, or they chose each other to his exclusion. He'd respect their decisions, heartrending as they could be.

"I will." Simon stood up. "I wish I had a better idea of where to go from here, but I feel better now that I've talked to you. I care about you a lot. I always will."

Darius thought back to their night in a dive hotel aboard a remote deep space substation the ship docked at for a spell on their way to New Eden. It was the first and last time in his recollection that they'd ever been separated from the rest of the group. His skin prickled with the memories of Simon's mouth on his body, what he could do . . .

"Do I want to know what you're thinking about that would cause that spike in your core temperature?" Simon asked.

"I'm sure you can guess."

Simon's breath caught. In the dim light, his pupils dilated, so slightly that anyone without enhanced vision would miss it. Darius couldn't help but feel a little smug at knowing what Simon had to be thinking about right now. Simon opened his mouth, seemed to reconsider his words, then closed it. Eventually, he said, "I'm going back to sleep."

"The pod, you mean."

"Yes. The pod next to mine is unoccupied."

Darius wasn't tired, but he wouldn't turn down an offer like that. It was a positive sign of things to come. "I think I'll take a nap, in that case."

He followed Simon out of the lounge. The lights cycled down when they left, plunging them into darkness. Night vision activated, they silently moved through the ship to the pods. Simon stepped into one and Darius into the one on his left. Before he could connect his wrists into the side ports, Simon reached over and covered his hand with his.

Darius's heart stuttered. The small touch sent a bolt of heat straight through him. He felt like a man dying of dehydration who had just been offered a glass of water.

All Simon said was a whispered, "Good night." Then he leaned back into his pod.

Darius would take it. He imprinted the touch, the sound of Simon's voice, into his memory bank before leaning back and closing his eyes.

———

THE MIRROR BOLTED to the wall opposite the bed had a glowing clock in its corner, telling Jasmine it was half-past six when she woke up. She sat up and stretched, pleasantly surprised at how normal she felt in the light of day.

She glanced through the porthole at the endless sea of black. Not quite light.

When she climbed out of bed, she found that her nausea was finally gone. She glanced at the spots where Darius had pressed the anti-nausea patch, still marveling at the technology. What other kinds of medicine did the cyborgs have? What would be waiting for them at the waystation? Jasmine had been jumping with excitement over the possibility of finally getting her hands on some new books and fresh paper that wasn't made by liquifying old stock. Now that she'd had a tiny taste of modern medicine, she wanted to look inside a hospital's closet and see what else could be treated. Or wherever hospitals kept their medication. She had never been to a proper one, with New Eden's now-destroyed clinic not holding much more than a few mild pain relievers distilled from the local flora.

She took a quick shower, luxuriating under the spray of hot water. Unsure of the etiquette surrounding water use in space, she only let herself enjoy it for a few minutes before reluctantly shutting it off. Then she dressed in a faded blue dress she'd worked over from an old one that had belonged to her mother, one of four changes of clothes she owned.

When she remembered how cold the ship was, relative to the toasty temperature she kept her cabin at, she slipped on her only sweater. She noticed the cuffs were fraying yet again and sighed. She'd lost count of the number of times she'd repaired it over the years. Without any sheep to provide wool, she had no way of making a new one. The last of New Eden's sheep had died following a weird illness six years prior.

Jasmine left her cabin, wondering if anyone else would be awake yet. She found Brandon, a cyborg who'd taken up residence with her friend Rodelle, in the lounge, a huge cup of something steaming in his hand. He brightened when he saw her. "How did you sleep?"

"Pretty good. What's that?" She nodded her head at the cup. "It smells good."

"Coffee, but it's from dehydrated cubes."

Jasmine could hardly believe her ears. "You really have coffee here?"

"Yeah, I missed it when we were on New Eden. We should bring some back."

"Can I have some?"

He looked at her like she was nuts for asking. "Of course. Do you know how to use the replicator?"

"Yeah. I just didn't think there would be coffee." She quickly crossed the room to the giant screen, which lit up at her touch. She tapped at the options that scrolled by until she landed on hot coffee, then placed the order.

"I guess it's been a long time since you had some," Brandon remarked.

"Try *never* had any. We had no way of growing it. I've

only ever read about it." She waited impatiently as the comp systems processed her request. The dispenser door slid open, revealing a steaming, fragrant mug the same size as Brandon's. She carefully removed it, then took a deep inhale of the heavenly aroma wafting off the dark brew. "Mmm."

"Wow, I didn't know. I guess the original colonists never bothered to cultivate it."

"Probably." Jasmine took a tentative sip. It was bitter, which she hadn't expected. She tried to compare it to another taste in her limited palette but came up blank. Bitter and strong, but not unpleasant. She understood how it could be an acquired taste for some.

"I'm sure I could find sugar or cream somewhere, if you'd like to add it to the coffee," Brandon offered.

She shook her head. "No, I want to try it this way. What's the point of watering it down?"

"Exactly. Don't say that around people who take their sweetener with coffee. They get snippy about it." Brandon grinned.

Jasmine took another swallow. Now that she knew what to expect from the taste, she didn't make a face. Its heat coursed through her, a pleasant feeling that perked her up like the books said it would. Maybe it was the placebo effect. "How can I bring some back to New Eden?"

"I'm sure we'll be able to get seeds to plant our own crops."

At that moment, she wished Hannah was here. She would know the right questions to ask about growing coffee —the best fields to plant it, the ideal growing conditions, soil quality. Jasmine's experience lay with textiles and crafts, skills much less important since the quake. She did know that the need for the caffeine fix she knew she was already acquiring wouldn't be as important as, say, wheat.

"At least the dehydrated coffee in your dispensers," she said.

"I'll make do with that until New Eden can grow or import its own."

Jasmine could hardly believe that the possibility of off-world imports was on the table. Before she could offer a rejoinder, Darius and Simon entered. Simon had lost that worried look he'd been sporting since before he kissed her—she felt giddy all over again at the memory—and Darius looked oddly more relaxed as well. They'd been stiff and formal in their interactions on New Eden, the polar opposite of what they were like with her alone. She'd wondered why they didn't have the same camaraderie the others shared. Being stuck together, cloned over and over again over the span of two centuries, tended to create bonds in ways Jasmine couldn't understand.

They gave each other a brief look that she couldn't decipher, one of affection and warmth. *Huh.*

They turned happy smiles in her direction. She had the distinct impression that if she wasn't here, they would have continued whatever conversation they'd started in the corridor. Maybe they still were, on their telepathic cybernetic link.

"Good morning," she said, breaking the silence.

Brandon curiously looked at all three and nodded but didn't comment.

"Morning to you too," Simon replied. "Jasmine, before we land at the waystation, you should probably have a checkup. You're bound to be exposed to new pathogens."

She hadn't expected the topic of conversation to veer in that direction. "Sure. Darius gave me a vaccine yesterday. I was expecting it to hurt."

"Why would you expect that?" asked Darius.

"They used to be done with shots. Syringes. I heard about them from my parents."

Darius and Simon glanced at each other, their expressions unreadable. "No one's used syringes in hundreds of years," Simon replied.

"Of course, no one has," Jasmine said. "Haven't we already established that any tech I might know about is outdated by centuries?"

"What about translators?" Simon asked.

Her interest was immediately piqued. "Like, a device I can wear? Hell, yeah, I want a translator!"

"Good, because the version of Standard you're speaking now isn't spoken anywhere else in the known galaxy, and there are a few other languages spoken on the waystation we're going to that you won't be familiar with. We're going to outfit you with a discreet translator you can hook around your tragus," Darius explained. Simon nodded in approval. Jasmine wondered what the hell was up with the two of them.

"We're due to arrive at the waystation in less than seventy-two hours, so you'll have plenty of time to try out the translator," Simon added.

In less than three days, Jasmine would be interacting with other species for the first time. She would be the first New Edener to contact others. *The first one off-world*, she silently corrected herself. Hannah had been the only person to run toward a ship breaking atmosphere in the middle of the night. In retrospect, that hadn't been the smartest thing to do, although it had worked out for them in the end.

Her excitement at being aboard an honest-to-God deep space waystation even eclipsed her curiosity about Simon and Darius. It was a feeling that was mixed with another, unfamiliar feeling. It took a few seconds for her to recognize it as jealousy.

She was jealous of their newfound closeness. God only knew why. She pushed it aside like errant threads on a garment she was reworking and stood up. "Let's get that translator."

CHAPTER FOUR

THE WAYSTATION they'd set a course for was the last stop on the way to nowhere. Or New Eden, Simon noted wryly, which was about ten stops past nowhere. Waystation 8305-C was owned and run by a cooperative who lived there full time, arranging imports for the sparse colonies in this part of the galaxy. The cooperative had built the station from the ground up a couple hundred years ago. In some ways, their goals weren't unlike the original New Eden settlers: the creation of a peaceful, self-sustaining colony. The waystation just happened to be successful at it.

Of course, the only reasons New Eden hadn't erupted into war were due to the lack of weaponry and its tiny population. Had its colony been more successful, the people could have been at each other's throats long before the earthquake ravaged it.

Jasmine had her face pressed against the viewport as the waystation came into view, nearly dislodging the translator hooked in her ear. She adjusted it over her tragus without tearing her eyes away from the waystation. The structure was a hulking mass of mismatched parts. Spiky turrets that once housed defenses stretched into nothingness, long abandoned for more efficient weaponry. Not that it was needed this far out; pirates couldn't be bothered to make the trip. The waystation nearly glowed from the lights dotted along its decks, a beacon of hope and civilization in deep space. The structure resembled a floating castle made of refuse, with new decks built on top of old ones. Docking bays jutted out on different levels, with little cohesion as to where they were built over the years. Shuttles and ships of varying sizes were attached to them. The sight had the strange effect of a mother animal feeding her young.

The waystation served anyone who paid their docking fees, powered down their weapons arrays, and behaved themselves onboard. The ship had notes in her comp systems from previous clone generations, warning them off of certain stations and planets in other regions of the galaxy, causing Simon to wonder if they'd pissed off the rest of the entire known universe over the decades. It explained why they'd terraformed an asteroid for their home instead of settling on a planet. And why all of their trade was restricted to tiny, obscure outposts like Waystation 8305-C.

"It's beautiful," Jasmine breathed against the viewport.

Simon blinked. The waystation looked like a squashed pile of metal. He tried to see it through her eyes. "Do you mean in an aesthetic sense or technical?"

"Why not both? It looks like a piece of what I'd imagine modern art looks like. And of course, the tech aspect of it is beautiful. I've never seen so many lights before!"

He squinted, but that only triggered his ocular enhancements to focus on a squished piece of turret. "I don't think I've ever been to an art gallery." The words slipped out before he could reconsider them.

"Me neither." She didn't sound despondent over the lack of culture. "Does the waystation have one?"

"I don't think so."

"Maybe some other time, when New Eden has its own spaceport and ship. I could fly somewhere and see them myself." There was a faraway note to her voice, as if mentally, she was already at the waystation, striding its main concourse. He wondered how long she had dreamed about leaving New Eden, seeing the stars. She hadn't peeled her eyes away from the waystation, now looming larger ahead.

The ship lurched forward a little as it came into the structure's orbit. A grinding noise sounded under them as its anchor clamps extended to lock on to one of the docking bays.

Darius, with his expert touch, guided the ship into the bay. Simon didn't have to leave the lounge or connect to their shared link to know Darius was in charge of the helm. He could've sworn that their vessel landed more comfortably when Darius was doing it, or maybe it was just his old infatuation at play. One that he was trying to put behind him.

He glanced at Jasmine, still wide-eyed with wonder as the ship glided forward. A thump reverberated through the ship as the waystation locked the ship's anchors into place. A faint, high-pitched whine sounded as an airlock tube latched on to the exterior door. When the noises stopped, Jasmine bolted from the lounge to the corridor. Unable to keep himself from smiling at her reaction, Simon followed her.

The exterior door was still tightly closed, its indicator

light flashing red. It paused, then shifted to yellow as the airlock tube's air recyclers activated. It finally glowed green, the color of safety. Simon pressed his palm into the door's biometric lock. It whirred for a few seconds, then the door cracked open with a faint hiss. Jasmine stood back and wrapped her arms around herself against the chill. She wore a drab gray shipsuit that had been created in the hard goods replicator. Its sleeves hung past her fingertips and the cuffs pooled around her ankles, but at least she was warm.

And *Darius* had made it for her. Jealousy and irritation flared in Simon when he thought of the two of them crowded around the galley replicator to see what the comp could generate. Simon should have been the one to think of that first.

He was with her now, he reminded himself. He'd be with her the first time she set foot on a deep space waystation.

"Wait for me!"

Hearing Darius's voice behind them, Simon's heart twisted. He and Jasmine turned around to see him, a wide smile across his face, revealing perfect white teeth. Something in Simon fluttered at the sight. His fellow cyborg had always had a great smile. It was what had drawn him to Darius in the first place. That, and his arms. The man's shoulders and back were truly something to behold. Works of art, albeit not the modern kind that Jasmine was so eager to see.

Simon forced a smile to his face. "Are you coming with us?"

"Of course!" Darius looked affronted at the suggestion that he would skip this. "I wouldn't miss strolling the concourse with you two for the world."

Simon felt oddly relaxed at the reply. With it, he felt a

corresponding pain. He missed Darius, what they'd once had.

He didn't know who he wanted more—Darius or Jasmine. It was a painful conundrum to be in.

Darius had already hauled open the exterior door all the way, revealing the airlock tube. It was an industrial gray, about three meters tall and wide, its floor scuffed from decades of use. Simon didn't realize there was a crowd behind them until the door was opened and they streamed through, leaving the three of them behind. "Let's go," said Darius, stepping into the airlock. "We have a lot of supplies to get, and I'm sure Jasmine wants to do some shopping."

She nodded eagerly.

Darius waited until Simon and Jasmine left the ship before taking a spot between them, a hand in the small of each of their backs. The touch felt electric, and Simon held back a shiver, trying not to give himself away. He glanced at Jasmine, whose eyes had gone huge. He couldn't tell why.

It felt right, oddly, but still unattainable.

———

GOD ABOVE, but Simon and Darius were being weird again. Jasmine sensed an odd, unfamiliar tension in the recycled air as they strode through the waystation's airlock. A blush rose to her cheeks as she imagined what it would be like to be between them in other circumstances, and . . .

She shook her head. Now was not the time to entertain those thoughts. Not when she was about to become the first New Edener to set foot on a deep space waystation.

She pushed aside her wayward thoughts as the airlock

gave way to a corridor, a grimy gray carpet runner underfoot. The corridor's overhead lights flickered, reminding Jasmine of the candles she used at home. A large, square-shaped metal frame waited ahead, which Darius walked right through. Seeing Jasmine hesitate, he said, "It's a weapons detector. The waystation doesn't allow anything like that aboard."

A frisson of nervousness slid along Jasmine's spine at the mention of weaponry. She should have considered the possibility of violence, considering who the cyborgs were and their reasons for existing, murky as they were. Their bodies had been manipulated and reproduced into weapons of war.

And here she was, about to march into an unknown waystation with no method of defense, except for her fists and screaming ability.

Simon placed a proprietary hand at the small of her back. The unexpected touch nearly burned her through her bulky shipsuit. Tingles radiated through her body. "I'll protect you against any boogeymen," he murmured into her ear.

"So will I," Darius vowed from her other side.

Oh, my. The spark Simon had ignited in her grew. Not for the first time, a flash of longing flared through her as she wondered what it would be like to be loved by both of them.

Stop torturing yourself. You're aboard an actual fucking space station. Enjoy it!

She wasn't sure if the chastising voice in her head was her own or Hannah's. Probably her own. Her ever-practical best friend would be rushing for the nearest spot that sold sacks of cattle feed or something before she would let herself enjoy a beer for the first time. Jasmine had never had one, but she hoped to try it during their stay. The only libation she'd ever had was sour-tasting dandelion wine.

At the end of the corridor, a giant circular door waited for them, its metal components gray and lightly rusting in some spots. A wave of bright green energy arced in the air before them, making Jasmine blink when it scanned along her eyes. A few seconds later, the door cycled open, ushering in a cacophony of noise.

"This is it," Simon said. "The waystation's main concourse."

Jasmine had to fight to keep herself from running into it. As it was, she moved faster than she had in recent memory, Simon and a chuckling Darius at her heels. She stopped in front of a fountain that stretched three meters into the air, streams of colored water spurting from its tall metallic columns dotted with holes. When she looked closer, she saw it wasn't water at all, but lasers. "Wow," she said, reaching out a hand.

"This is the first and only art installation on the waystation," Darius said.

"It isn't water," Jasmine replied. She turned her hand over in the light, marveling at the way it cut right through her.

"It's a controlled resource in deep space."

That made sense. She felt like an idiot for not considering that before making such an inane observation. New Eden had an overabundance of fresh water; it was one of the reasons the original settlers picked the planet in the first place.

She tore her gaze away from the light fountain to take in the surrounding sights. Vendors and stalls were lined up in rows, tightly pressed together, hawking everything from hardware she couldn't identify to food to . . . labor? She blinked, alarm threading through her. A blinking screen in the middle of the concourse advertised ship crew available for work. Names, qualifications, salary expectations, and contact details scrolled across it. Jasmine breathed a little easier. Not slave labor, then. Just be sure, she nudged Darius. "What's that?"

"I've heard it called the people board before. It's for employment."

"Like, *real* employment? No one's being sold?"

Darius looked affronted at the suggestion. "Not in this part of the galaxy."

"Good to know." A stall caught her eye near the people board, a hand-painted sign in front of it. The script sloped to the left, the symbols unfamiliar. They blurred together, and Jasmine blinked to clear to her vision. When she looked at the sign again, she saw it now read *Allion's Antiques and Ephemera.* It must have been her translator's doing, she decided, as wonderment at the technology had her freezing in her tracks. Behind it was a silver-haired elderly man and a rack of books. Her wonder quickly gave way to excitement. She grabbed Simon's arm, the person closest to her. "Oh, my God."

Something in her voice must have rattled him. "What?"

"There are *books* over there! Honest-to-God books!" Before she could reconsider, she bolted for the stall.

The old man behind it beamed at her reaction. This close, she could see that his skin bore scales along his throat and arms, exposed by his rolled-up sleeves. His eyes glowed yellow, the black irises narrow slits that widened at the sight of her. Jasmine forgot her voice for a second.

She was in the presence of someone who wasn't human.

Remembering her manners, she said, "Hello."

He nodded in response. "Good afternoon, my friend."

His voice held a serpentine hiss, and her translator crackled as it processed his words. When he breathed in, the tip of his forked tongue slipped between his lips, as if he was tasting the air.

Would it be rude to ask him what he was? Probably. "You have books," Jasmine said excitedly.

"I have many of the paper memorabilia of the past. Is there a particular title you are seeking?"

"Oh, no. I just like to read, is all. It's been so long since I had something new." She looked around the stall. It was little more than a counter in a self-contained box. Behind the proprietor was the shelf of books, displayed with their spines out. From the stall's ceiling, clear boxes holding beads, figurines, and other tchotchkes dangled from small hooks. "Do you have paper or pencils too?"

"I have both. It is so rare that someone wants them." He dug around under his counter, then produced a notebook with a pristine pink cover and a metal box.

Jasmine looked at them apprehensively. "May I?"

"Of course. See if it is to your liking."

With shaking hands, Jasmine opened the notebook's cover. She could scarcely contain her gasp at the sight of the crisp white pages. They were a little yellow around the edges from age, but that tiny flaw didn't bother her. She had never felt paper this smooth. It would be so much easier to draw and write on something so flawless. It was a far cry from the homemade paper made from pulped books and documents she'd had to make do with until the earthquake. There had been no point in making it after the disaster, when she'd lost all motivation to draw.

She opened the metal box to see a row of pencils in a plethora of colors, the ends sharpened to fine points. Longing filled her. She'd never wanted something so badly in her life.

As if he could read her mind, Darius whispered in her ear, "Do you want them?" She'd forgotten he was there. When she looked to her other side, she saw Simon, an unreadable expression on her face.

She nodded. "Yes."

"What about books?" Simon asked.

"Yes." The answer slipped out before she could stop herself out of politeness.

"Pick out some books. I'll take care of the purchase," Simon said to the proprietor.

"No, I can do that," Darius said.

"I really don't mind."

"Neither do I. I've had all this coin saved up and nowhere to spend it."

"We all have." There was an edge to Simon's voice.

"I draw too. You know that."

"I can share," Jasmine offered.

Darius raised a brow in response. Simon colored.

Jasmine's gaze flickered between them. There was a tension in the air she couldn't read. Had she caused a territoriality problem between them? "Um," she said uselessly. To the man behind the counter, she asked, "What kind of books do you have?"

"Everything you could imagine. My collection spans the galaxy and time."

That sounded delightful, but Jasmine needed more detailed information. "Like, do you have any fiction? Preferably in old Earth Standard or English?" Could he understand her language? She peered at his head, looking for a translator. A small white bead was pressed against his right earlobe, the scaled skin flat against his skull. Maybe that was it.

He tilted his head in surprise at her question. "I rarely get requests for Earth books."

"Do you have any?"

"But, of course." He lifted up a section of the counter on lubricated hinges. "Please step inside and see if I have anything that will please your tastes."

Jasmine stepped into the space, where she could see even more stuff hidden underneath the counter in the same clear boxes as those hanging from the ceiling. The proprietor rolled away the rack of books to reveal hundreds more on another rack behind it. This close, Jasmine could read the Earth titles. Excitement flowed through her. She glanced back at Darius and Simon on the other side of the counter, both of them watching her with an intensity that made her breath catch.

She turned back to the books, running her fingers over the spines. This was going to be fun.

CHAPTER FIVE

Darius trailed behind Simon and Jasmine, his arms laden down with packages. He didn't mind it; for one, both of them provided a nice view from the back, and he enjoyed their reactions. Simon seemed genuinely happy, and Jasmine delighted in everything around her. She darted from shop to stall to shop like one of the zip fish native to Leo-8. With her tangle of long blond hair that sparkled in the harsh lights overhead, she even resembled one of the shining creatures. At least she didn't have the razor-sharp teeth zip fish were known for, although Darius wouldn't turn down the chance for her to bite him.

Jasmine now lingered outside a stall that sold fabric and other sewing notions. She rubbed a few weaves between her fingers, a line worried between her brows as she assessed the quality. Catching up to them, Darius handed a few of her packages to Simon. "It's your turn. These are the light ones."

Simon took them without arguing. "What are you looking for? We can get a hard goods replicator on New Eden before long."

"Yeah, but doesn't that require a continuous power source and components we can't easily access?" Jasmine picked through an overflowing bin of mismatched scraps of all sizes. "We've been working and re-working old clothing and curtains for years. We're all tired of wearing threadbare things made from bedsheets. I can't tell you how long I've been dreaming of having new material to work with." She pulled out a piece of shimmering pink and gold fabric the size of a bedsheet and gasped.

"Put it on the pile," Darius said, nodding at his arms. He held her new books, some for herself and others for New Eden's children.

Jasmine surprised him when she shook her head and put it back in the bin. "It's too extravagant. We need practical materials." She nodded at piles of sturdy materials in neutral colors.

"It's a gift," Darius said.

"You said all of those are gifts. That's too many." She tapped the pile of books in his hands.

"You like to sew, don't you? You have the opportunity to make something beautiful for yourself. Get the fabric, Jasmine."

Indecision warred across her features. Simon raised an eyebrow at Darius.

"At least let us see what you look like after you've worked your magic with it," Darius added, putting what he hoped was a touch of suggestion into his voice.

Simon's brow nearly disappeared into his hairline.

An unreadable look passed over her face, but she grabbed the fabric and neatly folded it. "Only because you insisted," she said. She looked away, but not before Darius saw that her pupils had slightly dilated. He bit back a grin. He was sure she could create a sexy little number for herself from the delicate fabric.

Jasmine handed him the pink swath and turned back to the bolts in front of her. "Maybe something colorful, in case anyone else likes it," she murmured, audible only to anyone with enhanced hearing. She picked up a bolt of yellow and purple patterned material and stuck it under her arm as she hunted through the rest of the wares.

"What are you playing at?" Simon whispered in his ear. His friend's breath against his skin sent a warm shudder through Darius. He wondered if Simon remembered how the spot under his ear was one of his erogenous zones.

"Nothing." Darius pasted what he hoped was an innocent look on his face.

"Bullshit."

Irritation flared in Darius, replacing his good humor. Keeping his voice low and an eye on Jasmine rooting through notions on the opposite end of the shop, he said, "*I'm* getting tired of whatever angsty bullshit you're putting me and Jasmine through. I'm pretty sure this is how teenagers act." Not that Darius, or any of them, had encountered humanoid teenagers in their current state, but he vaguely remembered his original being one. "If you don't want to be with me, that's fine. I'm hurt, but I'll get over it. If you don't want to be with Jasmine, that's also fine, but you have to fucking tell her. I'm sick of this passive aggressive moping around New Eden and the ship." Darius didn't realize his voice was a low hiss until he finished speaking.

Simon stared at him, shocked into silence. At last.

Jasmine returned to them, arms full of thread and sealed packs of sewing supplies. "Everything okay?" she asked, looking between them.

Darius nodded.

"Just fine," Simon bit out.

Remorse flooded through Darius at Simon's reply, at

the anguish in his voice. *I'm sorry,* he said over their shared link. Simon's had been closed to everyone for days, and Darius didn't know if he would receive it.

To his surprise, Simon replied, *It's nothing.*

When Simon spoke aloud, his voice was brittle in its artificial cheerfulness. "Hungry?" Simon asked. "Or thirsty?"

Jasmine nodded. "Yeah. Are you sure you two are all right?"

"Peachy," Simon replied. "I'll settle our account here and meet you on the concourse."

———

THE WAYSTATION HAD public gardens on an upper deck, a manmade masterpiece of greenery. The space was more than two square kilometers, filled with trees and shrubs from across the galaxy. A connected path of streams and ponds ran around the space, filled with small gold and black fish native to the Perseus Sector. There were a few woodland critters here and there, all lifelike androids, their programming ensuring they were always happy to be played with. At 1900 hours, the artificial sky glowed in a pink and orange sunset.

Jasmine loved it. As soon as they walked into it, she'd taken off like a child in a candy shop, her reaction undoubtedly enhanced by the half-glass of beer she'd tried at a concourse drink kiosk. Simon lingered behind her with Darius while she ran ahead, eager to see everything she could before the ship departed later that evening. Everything they'd come for was safely stored in the cargo bays. In a few days, New Eden would be on its way to finally having a fully working communications tower for the first time in decades. Much-needed building supplies were also carefully stacked in one of the bays. New Eden's substandard housing would be improved at last.

Simon thought about the row of dilapidated houses where Jasmine's home was. The few still-standing structures were barely intact, missing windows, and their plumbing that had been hastily slapped together was now falling apart. All it would take was another tremor for them to fall down. Simon's heart clenched at the mere thought of Jasmine being hurt.

"What are you thinking about?"

Darius's question brought him back to his senses. Jasmine had disappeared over a hill, chasing an AI hare, giving them some privacy for a few minutes. "What's waiting for us back at New Eden."

"I like how you said 'us.'"

An irritated retort was on the tip of his tongue, but Simon stopped himself in time. He was tired of arguing with Darius, tired of being short and rude with him and Jasmine, the two people he cared most about in the universe. Still, he chose his words carefully. "I don't know what we are. I don't know how the rest of the crew would react to our relationship."

"You think our crew would care about what a couple of consenting adults get up to in private?" Darius lightly nudged him in the ribs.

"They wouldn't care. Rhys didn't when I told him."

"You went around telling Rhys all the dirty details?" Darius didn't sound angry, just surprised.

Simon felt himself blush. "Not the specifics. Just that I care about you and Jasmine in ways I've never felt before, and I'm not sure how to handle that." He kept his gaze schooled on the dirt trail ahead of him, looking for Jasmine. She'd come back soon enough, or they'd catch up with her.

"I really think you should talk to her. Or we can do that together." To illustrate his point, Darius reached for Simon's hand.

Even a few hours ago, Simon would have pushed him away. Now, he welcomed the touch, squeezing Darius's, as if to make sure he wouldn't run off after Jasmine.

They walked hand-in-hand for a few minutes. An artificial breeze floated by, perfumed with a fragrance Simon's cybernetics told him was lily of the valley. It was pleasant, anyway. A pair of little boys ran past them, heedless of everything but the antigrav ball they chased. A moment later, a woman who shared their matching shock of bright yellow hair and faint silvery scales on her exposed neck and wrists strolled by, nodding at them in greeting. "*Sorzjan!*" she called after the boys. Diloran for "Wait up." Much of the waystation's permanent residents were Diloran or human-Diloran descendants. Simon thought about the Diloran merchant who had sold Jasmine all her beloved books, now waiting for her in her cabin aboard the ship.

They still couldn't see Jasmine, but Simon wasn't worried about her. Judging from Darius's saunter, he wasn't either. "I meant it when I said I'd talk to her with you," Darius said quietly.

"And what would I tell her? The two of us had a, well, I'm not sure what it was, and I'm also crazy for her and you at the same time? How does that work? I'm bad enough at this as it is, without adding a third person into it."

"She likes us both. I'm not so sure she would shut down the way you think she might."

Simon stopped in the path, brown dirt swirling around his boots. He pinched the bridge of his nose between his fingers, an old habit of his that came out when he was frustrated. A voice in the back of his mind wondered if his original had done that too. Probably, he decided. "Did you miss the part where I said I'm bad at this?"

"I'm pretty sure all of us are. Although, I'm actually sort of impressed that a bunch of cloned cyborgs can be so repressed themselves yet so accepting of other people and their choices. I wouldn't worry about what the others might think about us. The worst case-scenario is apathy."

Simon knew that. He wasn't afraid of people knowing about their relationship, so much as others knowing about it and watching it implode when he fucked it up. Plus, there was also the matter of all of them having to work and live together. "I don't have a blueprint for this."

"Now you sound like Rhys, and I don't want to do to him what I want to do to you. And Jasmine," he quickly added.

"Together?"

"If you two would let me."

Heat flared through Simon at the suggestion, and for a few seconds, he couldn't speak.

Darius chuckled, a low, throaty sound that had every nerve in Simon's body on fire. He knew that laugh, remembered it from when they were in bed during their first and only night together. He didn't know until now how much he'd wanted to hear it again. "Darius," he said softly, reaching for his hands again. He clasped them between his, needing the contact. He leaned forward, Darius's familiar scent of soap and skin both comforting and electrifying.

He didn't know who moved first, but their lips met, tentatively at first. It was as if Darius was afraid Simon would bolt like one of the skittish artificial animals skipping around the grounds. Simon leaned into him, wanting more, and Darius was only too happy to give it. Simon's hands traveled up Darius's arms, bringing him closer . . .

"Um."

It took all of .0087 seconds for Jasmine's voice to register. Both of them pulled apart and stood side by side, arms touching. Simon's lips still burned from the kiss, body throbbing with need that he would have to ignore again.

He didn't know how to feel. Judging by the look on Jasmine's face, she didn't either. She looked like she wanted to say something, opening her mouth and closing it. "Did you know there's a swimming hole over that hill?" she asked.

He did. So did Darius. They had enjoyed a quick dip in it the last time the ship was at the waystation. "Yes," Simon said evenly.

"Then I guess there's no point in you seeing it again."

"Jasmine . . ." Darius's voice was soft, a tone Simon had only ever heard when they spoke together in private. Despite the gravity of the situation, a shiver of pleasure rippled down his spine.

"No." She crossed her arms over her chest. "I'm not going to ask questions, but this explains a lot. I'm not mad," she quickly added.

"Maybe we could . . ."

"Nah," she said. "I'd rather go back to the ship. I think you said it would be loaded up with everything by now?"

Simon nodded. "It's ready to break dock whenever we get back."

"Then, let's go." Without waiting for an answer, Jasmine briskly walked ahead of them, dust trailing behind her.

———

JASMINE DIDN'T SAY anything the rest of the walk back to the ship, nor could she bring herself to look at Simon or Darius. Heat suffused her entire body, a combination of anger and . . . arousal? She felt herself flush when she thought about the two of them locked in that embrace, clear adoration across each of their features.

It explained so much about why Simon had been standoffish with her. But questions still lingered, tumbling through her mind. How long had this been going on? Did the other cyborgs know? Where did she fit into this mess? Damn them. She couldn't even enjoy the concourse's sights on the way back to the docks.

Why hadn't Simon said anything to her? All their flirting, all their little touches, that kiss—she willed away her tears of humiliation. Of loneliness. She was tired of being alone. At least she had some new books to while away her hours and brand-new fabric to outfit New Eden with clothing. She wouldn't have to nurse her broken heart without distractions.

Damn them for ruining her first trip into space. Damn them for ripping her heart in half. And damn herself for opening up to the possibility of ever finding love or affection with someone.

Once aboard the ship, she made a beeline for her cabin, noting that no one followed her. Only in its relative safety did she throw herself on the bed and weep into the pillow.

CHAPTER SIX

"You want to tell me what the hell happened on the waystation that made Jasmine run away like the proverbial bat out of hell?" Brandon asked. He leaned against the pilot's seat, the navigation panel before him. Not that it was needed, when a cyborg could set a course with his mind if he was connected to the ship. Of all of them, Brandon had embraced his human side the fastest once they reached New Eden. He enjoyed his humanity far more than the others.

Especially Simon, at this point. How he wished he could shut off his emotions like some of his previous clones had. He couldn't remember all the details, but he had the vague notion that someone had rebelled and said *no more to emotion dampening* a couple of generations ago.

"None of your business," Darius replied before sinking into another seat. Simon gave him a look that he hoped questioned Darius's intelligence. They had come to the bridge for privacy. They wouldn't have that with Brandon present.

Brandon looked between them, one dark eyebrow raised. "Should I make myself scarce?"

"Please," Simon replied wearily.

"There's nowhere else on the whole fucking ship for you two to talk? Spare cabin, the lounge, the pods?"

"He has a point," Darius said.

"Nah, I'm fucking with you." Brandon stood and stretched. "If you two are going to stay dropped out of the communal signal, could you keep an eye on the course?"

"Any ion storms brewing on the way back to New Eden?" Darius asked.

"No, and no unfriendlies, either. Not that I'd expect to see any in this part of the galaxy. Don't forget to say you're sorry to Jasmine." He left the bridge without waiting for Simon to offer a retort.

Once he was gone, Simon sank into the empty pilot's seat. "Well, at least she knows," he said miserably.

"As if we could forget to apologize to her," muttered Darius, uncharacteristically morose.

"What do we do next?"

"You know how I feel. Per one of the books I leafed through at that stall, I'd happily bang both of you like a screen door in a hurricane."

Simon felt himself flush, arousal thrumming through him, body stiffening. He thought about their night together in a cheap hotel room on a deep space substation even more remote than the one they were leaving. How it had been a culmination of weeks of sly touches, longing looks, the realization that Simon was in lust with him in a way he never expected to experience in his enhanced form. Even then, before their resettlement on New Eden, Darius had been more in touch with his human side than any of them.

When he found his voice, all he could ask was, "How do we say that to her?"

Darius shifted, face brightening at the question. "I'm glad you're seeing this from my perspective." He shifted forward in his seat, closer to Simon. When he spoke, his voice had the darker, sensual undercurrent that set all Simon's senses on alert. "Are you going to tell me you've never thought about it? Both of us?"

Simon had hardly dared to think of that scenario. "Not exactly."

"It's not nice to lie to me."

Simon tried to keep himself from visibly shuddering in pleasure. "I'm not."

"Not even a little? You've never thought about what it might be like to have both of us in your bed?"

"If I thought about that too much, I might explode, and I have enough shit to deal with."

Darius's chuckle was low in his ear. He lightly nipped Simon's earlobe, teeth scraping against his skin. Damn it, he really did know how to push every one of Simon's buttons. And if Simon didn't put a stop to it now, he and Darius would end up tangled together on the deck, heedless of the others strolling in. Or Jasmine. That would be the worst of all, if that happened before they could speak to her.

"We have to speak to Jasmine now," Simon said, nearly hating the words as he spoke them. "She deserves that."

Darius released a decidedly unsexy sigh and leaned back against his seat with a little more drama than necessary. "I know."

"Now, before we return to New Eden." Simon rose, then held out his hand for Darius to haul him to his feet.

"What about the others? Should we tell them about us?"

Simon had thought about that since their arrival on New Eden. "I don't think it would make things weird with the crew now that we have New Eden. We aren't in such close quarters anymore. I don't know what we would tell them, though." He almost said, *we aren't in a relationship*, but stopped himself in time. He wasn't sure what they were yet, nor did he want to hurt Darius more than he already had.

To his surprise, Darius took that statement in stride. "We have time to figure it out." He raised his hand and traced a finger along Simon's pulse, starting at the sensitive spot under his ear and trailing along his throat to his black shipsuit's collar. Simon leaned into him, wanting more, pressing a kiss to Darius's cheek. Despite the chasteness of it, Darius's breath caught. "Let's go find Jasmine."

It wouldn't be difficult. Simon's internal comp told him she was in her cabin.

Once there, he pressed the chime beside the door. "We should have brought something for her," Darius muttered. "Flowers or something."

"Where would we get flowers?"

"I'm sure we could program one of the replicators to create a bouquet."

The door slid open. Jasmine stood before them, eyes puffy and ringed with dark shadows, but she wasn't crying. Her lips thinned at the sight of them, and with it, Simon's heart lurched. "What do you want?" she asked.

"Can we come in?" Darius asked.

"It's your ship. You can do whatever you want."

"It's *your* cabin," Simon corrected her. "You don't have to let us in if you don't want to."

"We want to talk to you," Darius added.

She gave a half shrug and stepped aside. "Come on in. I'm sure this will be good," she said sarcastically. She sat down on the bed, hands clasped in front of her.

Simon and Darius exchanged a quick look before

Darius took a seat on the bed next to her. Even though Simon wanted to do the same, he didn't want her to feel like they were trapping her in. Not that he didn't *want* her between them that way, but . . . he swallowed. His imagination was getting away from him at the worst possible time. He unclipped one of the chairs from its deck lock and hauled it to the bed, sitting in front of both of them.

Jasmine's gaze flicked between them. "So, I guess you two are a thing."

"Sort of," Simon replied, just as Darius said, "Simon would call it complicated."

"We're here to apologize for not being upfront with you in the first place," Darius said.

"You weren't the one who kissed me. You don't owe me anything," Jasmine said, glaring at Simon.

"It's not that I didn't want to kiss you. I just didn't have the opportunity," Darius said.

A line furrowed between her brows. "What?"

"Jasmine, I'm sorry," Simon said. "I've had feelings for Darius for a long time, and I've had them for you since we met."

"You have?" Jasmine looked at Darius. "What about you?"

Don't be crude, Simon told Darius through their link. Darius winked at him in response.

"You're talking to each other in your heads. That isn't fair in this situation," Jasmine complained.

Deflated, Simon knew she was right. "Of course not. I apologize for that too. I told Darius not to be crude, like he was on the bridge."

"What do you mean?"

"He's talking about how I told him I'd bang both of you like a screen door in a hurricane, which is what I said when we were figuring out how to talk to you about this."

"Exact words," Simon added.

"I'm pretty sure it's an old world idiom. I picked it up in one of your books. I'm not sure I've ever even seen a screen door."

"Some of the falling down buildings on New Eden have them," said Jasmine. As if the import of Darius's words finally sank in, she blushed. "You said that?"

"I did. I like you both," Darius said. "More than like."

"Oh. Okay." She looked down at her hands, still clasped in her lap, but not before Simon saw her pupils had dilated again. He thought about her reaction to them on the concourse, with the pile of pink fabric in her hands.

He and Darius didn't speak, waiting for Jasmine to do so. Finally, she said, "Simon, you were the second person I've ever kissed."

He hadn't been expecting that. "Oh?"

"You may have noticed the lack of men on New Eden. I kissed a boy when I was a kid, and he passed away a couple of years later from a fever." She shook her head a little, a rueful smile on her face. "Look, I don't want to talk about him or illness. I can't believe we're talking about *this*."

"Should we go?" Simon asked.

"No. I'm not—well, I'm not opposed to *this*." She gestured at the two of them. Hope flared in Simon. "I'm just a little overwhelmed by it."

Simon was still reeling from the news that he was the second person she'd ever kissed. He felt like an idiot for not thinking about that before; New Eden's population was tiny, and she was right about the lack of eligible men. Of course, she would be inexperienced. So was he, or at least his current iteration was. "I'm overwhelmed by this too," he admitted.

"What's up with you two?" she asked. "I don't think that's an unreasonable question to ask."

"It isn't," Simon agreed. Taking a chance, he moved from the chair to the bed next to her. Catching Darius's bemused expression, he said, "I'm sure I don't have to explain what it's like when you're living with a small group of people and everyone knows everyone else's business."

"I thought you guys were bonded and shit," Jasmine replied.

"Some of us better than others," Darius said dryly.

Simon smiled. "We are. We're bound together by our cybernetics and circumstances in a way I can't explain to someone who isn't enhanced."

"And that's the problem," Jasmine translated.

"Yes. It makes romantic entanglements complex."

Darius snorted. "Is that what you're calling it?"

"Do you have a better idea?"

"If I had some time, I could probably think of a few other, hotter, terms." Darius's voice had taken on that darker quality again that always drove Simon crazy. He had to be doing it on purpose.

"At least you can get away from someone on New Eden," Simon continued. "You have your own houses. You have space to walk and think."

"And if a couple of cyborgs are having an affair, it could make things weird with the rest of the crew," Jasmine said. "I get it. I still wish you'd told me sooner."

Simon took another chance and reached for her hands. To her relief, she unclenched them and let him thread his fingers through hers. She was warm, bordering on hot, and the sensors in his palms and fingertips told him that her heart rate was elevated. So was his. "I didn't know how. I was trying to figure out how I could be with only one of you when I didn't want to give up the other. I've never done a relationship before. I'm pretty bad at it so far."

"What about your previous clones?"

"I don't go rooting through their memories."

"I see."

Darius reached for her other hand, the gesture tentative. She slid her fingers over the back of his before taking it. "I thought I would have to make a choice too," she said, voice quiet.

Simon had to force himself to breathe. "Why?"

"I liked you both. I still do. I wouldn't want to hurt the other if I had to pick one of you."

Simon's eyes met Darius's over the top of Jasmine's head. "You don't have to do that if you don't want to," Darius said.

Darius's voice seemed to have the same effect on her as it did on Simon. A faint shiver slid down her body. "That just makes this a new kind of complicated," she whispered.

"Complicated can be fun," Darius murmured.

Simon breathed deeply, the scents of Jasmine and Darius flooding his overwhelmed senses. He shifted, trying to get in a comfortable position to ease some of the ache on his cock. He didn't have to ask Darius to know he was as overwhelmed with lust as he was. Simon leaned closer to her, white-blond hair tickling his nose.

"I think Simon wants to kiss you again," Darius said.

"More than that," Simon murmured into her hair. To Jasmine, he asked, "May I?"

"Yes," she whispered, turning her face up to him.

Simon's lips fastened over hers, his tongue demanding entrance. She gasped against his lips, then immediately responded, hands reaching to twine around his neck. Dimly, he was aware of Darius's low chuckle and the rustle of fabric as Simon moved closer on the bed behind her.

Simon's hands slid to her hips, pulling her closer against him. Without breaking their kiss, she adjusted her position so she could lean into him. She lightly sucked on his lower lip, causing his breath to stutter. He pulled away so he could catch his breath, then tucked a strand of hair behind her ear. Her color was high, lips swollen. He thought she'd never looked more beautiful.

Over her shoulder, Darius said, "May I?"

Her eyes widened and she looked over at him. "May you what?" There was a teasing note to her voice, one Simon already liked.

Darius brushed aside her hair and lightly kissed her neck, drawing a mewl from her. She shifted so she could better see his face, and Simon gripped one of her hands, needing to keep their own connection too. Darius tilted her face to his, mouth crashing down on hers in the possessive way Simon loved so much. Instead of being jealous, as he'd worried he might be, Simon instead found the sight unbearably hot. He wanted her to enjoy being with Darius as much as he did.

Darius pulled away just enough that both of them could see the dazed expression on Jasmine's face. To Simon, he said, "Your turn."

Simon was only too happy to oblige. He lowered his face to hers, dusting her cheek with tiny kisses that made her gasp. He slid his hands around her waist, silently damning the shipsuit's bulky material that kept him from touching her skin. When he reached her mouth, he lightly sucked at her lower lip the way she had done to him, wanting to give her the same pleasure she'd given him.

It worked. She arched into him, wanting more, and he was only too happy to oblige.

He pulled away just enough to meet her gaze. With shaking fingers, he reached for the seal on her shipsuit, lightly tugging where it began on the neckline. It split apart a few centimeters, revealing tanned skin. A hint of her faded yellow and white striped tank top appeared. Not for the first time, Simon wondered if the tan was all over. New Eden had plenty of private spots to lie in the sun.

Before he could ask, Jasmine opened the seal the rest of the way until the suit pooled around her hips. Her nipples formed hard points under the shirt, making Simon itch to take it off her.

She looked at him and Darius in turn, as if deciding what to do next. Taking a deep breath, she pushed the suit off her hips, kicking it to the deck. She wore a pair of utilitarian underwear beneath, not that Simon cared about that. He doubted Darius did, either. Haloed in the cabin's soft light, she looked like an old world erotic artwork come to life.

To his surprise, she balled her hands into fists in her bare lap and gave a nervous little laugh. "What happens next?" she asked.

"Whatever you want," Darius replied.

She colored again, although Simon suspected it had to do with embarrassment as much as arousal. "I've never done this before, let alone with two people," she confessed.

"I haven't had sex with two people before, either, and not with a woman," Simon admitted.

Darius reached for her, brushing his hand across her chest. "I'm pretty sure we can figure things out as we go along," he murmured in her ear. He slid a hand under her tank top, raising the hem to trail his fingers across her bare abdomen.

Simon reached for her leg, trailing his fingertips from her knee along her inner thigh. The sensors implanted in them sent little shocks of pleasure up his arm with the motion. On an impulse, he activated his sensors into analysis mode, causing them to offer tiny vibrations along her skin, stopping just before he reached her underwear. She gave an unexpected cry at the sensation, drawing a smirk of satisfaction from Darius. Simon probably had the same expression on his face. "Tell us what you want," he whispered into her ear.

CHAPTER SEVEN

IF JASMINE HADN'T BEEN SUPPORTED by Simon and Darius on either side of her, she might have collapsed against the mattress. Her breathing quickened, and even though she no longer wore her borrowed shipsuit, her sleeveless top and underwear felt like too much clothing. Goose bumps popped along her skin. She wasn't sure if they were due to the ship's crisp, recycled air or the two of them surrounding her. Instead of feeling claustrophobic, she felt oddly secure. Safe. She knew if she called everything off and told them to leave, they would.

Not that she wanted them to leave. She wanted to give in to the secret fantasies she'd been harboring since both of them began shamelessly flirting with her. She just wasn't sure where to begin. At least they were new at this too.

"It's not fair that I'm the only one undressed," she complained.

"Definitely not," Simon agreed. Without another word, he unsealed his form-fitting black suit, the sleeves retracting into the shoulders. Jasmine watched, fascinated both by the tech and his body. She'd seen him shirtless while working under the sun a few times, but it was something else altogether to see him up close. His muscles bunched under the metal plates embedded in his pectorals and arms. The flat plane of his stomach trembled when she experimentally ran her hand over it, dipping under his suit's fabric where it bunched around his hips.

"Beautiful, isn't he?" Darius said into her ear, his breath sending a shiver down her spine.

"Yeah." Her mouth went dry.

"You should see him when he's all worked up." Darius stroked her bare thigh in a movement reminiscent of Simon's earlier caress. It was distracting her from looking at the bulge at Simon's front. She didn't know which to concentrate on. Simon ran his hand over his erection, just once, a strained look on his face.

"What about you?" she asked Darius.

"I want you, too. But I think Simon had designs on you first, and he's been waiting a long time for this."

Heat radiated in tingles through her body, pooling between her legs. The dull throb there that had been aching since they sat on either side of her was becoming unbearable. She was desperate for a climax to happen soon. "Yes," she said breathlessly.

"Take off your shirt," Simon ordered. "I want to see all of you."

The first seed of doubt planted itself in Jasmine's mind as she reached for her shirt hem. What if she didn't meet their expectations? They had to have seen plenty of beautiful women along their travels. How would she compare?

You're being ridiculous. They're already here and have made it clear they want to fuck you, no matter what.

She pulled her top over her head, baring her breasts for them. Leaning back on the bed, she tried to look and feel like the siren they thought she was. Any insecurity she felt about her appearance melted away under the heat of their appreciative gazes.

Simon pushed the rest of his suit down his hips and legs, kicking it away. His freed cock jutted out, larger than Jasmine expected. Then again, she'd never been in the presence of a naked man before. She hadn't known what to expect.

"What do you think?" Darius asked, eyes not leaving Simon's body. Simon's hand traveled down his stomach to grip his erection, lightly stroking it while he looked at Jasmine, his eyes hooded with lust.

"Wow," she whispered. She wasn't sure how it would fit inside her.

Darius's voice rumbled in her ear, a low purr. "I concur. Here's my suggestion for what to do next. Both of us want to do unspeakable things to you, but Simon has been pining over you for weeks now, and I think he staked his claim first."

Jasmine thought about the kiss in the lounge, then about the notion of someone putting a claim on her. She should be bothered by the suggestion. Instead, it was a strange comfort to have them doing that. It felt *right*.

"There's something I'd like to do to you first, if you want," Darius continued. He traced his fingers along her breast. He lightly tweaked her nipple between two of them, drawing another cry from her. "Then I think Simon has to fuck you before he explodes."

"I think I might too," she whimpered when he pinched her other nipple.

He rose, then knelt before her on the deck. He pulled her closer to the edge of the bed, then eased her thighs apart. Jasmine had a pretty good idea of what he intended to do next, and a shiver of anticipation raced through her. "Lie back," Darius said. The words were a command she was only too happy to obey. He hooked his thumbs in the waistband of her underwear, then slid it down her legs. Spreading her farther, he regarded her naked sex with a look of reverence. When she was able to tear her gaze away from him to look at Simon, he looked serious, invested in her pleasure.

When Darius finally put his lips on her, she nearly arched off the bed. Her hands fisted in his hair, urging him to continue, and with a growl, he did. His hands gripped her thighs as he delved in, tongue exploring her folds until he found her already sensitized clit. At her cry of pleasure, one of his hands snaked around her thigh to her entrance, pushing one finger inside her with a gentleness she hadn't expected. With agonizing slowness, he slid it in and out of her, testing her limits, before adding a second finger. He increased his pace with his hand and tongue until Jasmine felt the first wave of her orgasm crashing over her. She welcomed it, riding against Darius's face until she was wrung out and limp on the bed.

Darius lightly bit her inner thigh, coaxing a squeak of pleasure from her, then withdrew his fingers. Rising to his full height, he grabbed Simon by the waist, kissing him. "I think she's ready for you," he said. Jasmine's breath caught at the sight of them together. Darius winked at her, then stripped off his suit. "Are you?" he asked.

She nodded. Her fatigue forgotten, she scooted farther back on the bed, excitement rising again. "Come here," she said to Simon, hoping she sounded as seductive as she hoped to.

Simon crawled across the bed, looming over her. He leaned down, trailing hot kisses along her collarbone, over her breast, then took a nipple into his mouth. With his free hand, he teased her other breast before tracing a path down her stomach to her soaked and aching center, plunging two fingers inside her the way Darius had. Jasmine cried out again, her earlier nerves about him being inside her waning. "You feel good," he murmured against her skin before taking her other breast into his mouth.

The bed sank as Darius lay down next to them. He turned on his side, propping himself up on one elbow, his other hand wrapped around his cock. He stroked himself as he watched them, breaths coming faster. Jasmine watched in fascinated lust for a few seconds, then turned to the man over her, kneeling between her legs, his own erection in his hand. Jasmine reached for it, sliding her hand up and down the way Darius was doing to himself. Simon threw back his head, sucking in a harsh breath. "Like that," he said through clenched teeth.

Beads of fluid gathered at the tip, and she idly wondered what it would taste like. Before she could find out, Simon positioned himself at her entrance, gently pushing forward. Her eyes widened, and her previous thoughts about him fitting inside her faded. She lay back against the mattress and tried to relax.

He slowly pushed forward, taking his time. Jasmine held her breath, watching as he sank a little inside her, then looking at Darius, whose look of concentration was almost as intense as Simon's. Through it, Darius gave her an encouraging look, as if to reassure her that she could do this, could take him.

With one thrust, Simon was fully seated inside her. Jasmine gasped at the heady mix of pleasure and pain, feeling like she might be split in two if she moved. She tried to catch her breath and adjust to the feeling of him inside her, wiggling her hips as she did so. Simon nearly lost his balance over her, biting out a muffled, "Fuck!"

Darius's murmured in her ear, "Are you all right?"

Jasmine nodded, quickly meeting his eyes. There was concern there, mixed in with lust. "Yes."

Darius pressed a kiss to her temple. "Good." To Simon, he said, "Be gentle."

Simon's voice was strained when he replied. "Of course." He almost sounded affronted at the notion that he might not be. He withdrew from her, then thrust into her again. It was easier to take this time, and Jasmine moved her hips to meet his thrust when he did it again. Instinctively, she wrapped one leg around his hip, drawing him deeper inside her. It encouraged him, and he increased his pace, driving into her with his hands braced on either side of her head. He leaned down to kiss her, tongue as forceful as he was inside her. Jasmine's other leg twined around his hip, her hands gripping his back so hard, she thought her nails might leave marks. Beside them, Darius's low grunts sounded in her ear as he stroked himself.

Simon adjusted his angle, pushing deeper inside her and hitting something that ignited a new fire in her. She was going to come again. "Keep doing that," she said, voice breathy. It was hard to speak. Simon doubled his efforts, doing as she said, reaching between their bodies with one hand to stroke her clit. "*God!*"

Darius made a vague noise of approval. Simon's pace increased, and Jasmine could feel her climax building, whimpers of pleasure caught in her throat. As it slammed into her, she bit into Simon's shoulder to muffle her scream. Simon didn't stop, pounding into her, muscles bunching under her hands. "I—so good," he bit out. "I'm going . . ."

She knew what he was about to do. He came inside her with a howl, heat filling her, the cords on his neck standing out in stark relief. Beside them, Darius's hand moved faster and faster until his own orgasm spilled over him, eyes never leaving her and Simon, where their bodies were joined.

With a final gasp, Simon leaned down on his elbows, his face a couple of centimeters away from hers. His eyes were glassy, and she knew hers had to be the same. When she glanced at Darius, he looked sated, his breaths still coming fast.

Simon pressed a sloppy kiss to her lips. "You feel so fucking good."

"So do you." She wiggled her hips, acutely aware of his cock still inside her.

Darius tilted her face so he could kiss her, then Simon. "That was incredible to watch."

As amazing as it felt with Simon inside her, Jasmine felt a little selfish. "Was it good for you?" she asked curiously.

He sank against the pillows. "Fuck, yes."

"Do you want to do it too?" she asked Darius. As if to punctuate her point, Simon flexed inside her before withdrawing from her body. She immediately felt his loss.

"So soon? Wasn't that your first time?" Darius asked. He pulled her closer to him, and she turned on her side to face him. Simon settled on her other side, spooning her, hand resting on her hip.

"Yeah." Now that she thought about it, she realized she was a little sore. "Maybe we should wait a little."

Darius kissed her. "We have time."

Simon reached for the blanket bunched at the foot of the bed, draping it over them as their skin cooled. He kissed her shoulder, hand reaching across her body for Darius's. As Jasmine fell into a light sleep between them, she thought there could be no better place in the universe to be.

CHAPTER EIGHT

THE SHIP BROKE New Eden's atmosphere before dawn, reminding Darius of their first approach to the planet. He remembered the rest of the crew's trepidation, unsure if the low-tech population who sent out the desperate SOS so many months ago would be welcoming to a group of cloned cyborgs. Darius had been secretly looking forward to their new life, certain the New Edeners would accept their help in exchange for a new home. He'd also harbored a longing to pick up with Simon publicly, at least until he'd met Jasmine.

He was grateful he didn't have to choose between them, that they didn't choose each other to his exclusion. As the ship descended into the open field, he wondered when they would be amenable to telling others about them. Well, Brandon already knew. The other cyborg was nothing if not discreet and would keep it to himself. He, Simon, and Jasmine hadn't had any privacy since their interlude in Jasmine's cabin, instead helping to sort through the piles of supplies in the cargo bays before the ship returned.

The other cyborgs who'd joined them—FH22, CW44, Brandon, and Justin—were now assembled on the bridge with them as the ship descended. Jasmine, strapped into a seat, looked giddy as the ship's heavy air engine engaged. Darius hoped she would never tire of space travel. He loved seeing that wondrous look on her face, among other expressions.

He couldn't help but smirk when he thought of how she looked in the throes of passion. He was looking forward to having scratch marks on his back to match Simon's one day. Darius ordinarily wasn't a jealous man, but he was envious of Simon wearing evidence of Jasmine's passion.

Jasmine didn't get up until the ship had landed, then rose on shaky legs. Simon was immediately next to her, helping her stay upright as she readjusted to being on solid ground. She stumbled over her first few steps, then bounded to the airlock, waiting for the exterior door to open.

In a scene reminiscent of their first landing, Hannah Forsyth waited outside. This time, Rhys stood next to her. Jasmine squealed in delight and ran down the ramp to envelop her in a fierce hug. "Oh, my God!" she yelped. "It was incredible!"

Hannah squeezed back. "I missed you. I had no idea you were going to run off. Don't scare me like that again!"

Jasmine pulled away. "I was fine. I was in great hands." She looked behind her at Darius and Simon, blond brows lifted at their private innuendo. If Rhys or Hannah noticed, neither of them gave any indication.

"We have so much stuff," Jasmine said excitedly. "We can rebuild the comm tower so much faster than we thought! And there are building supplies to make the existing structures quake-proof. We can rebuild the landing pad and infirmary, oh! I have books too!"

"So many books," said Simon.

"And fabric. We can finally stop sewing old curtains into clothes. I can start doing textiles again! Maybe we can get the old loom fixed soon too."

"What about medicine?" Hannah asked.

"We have sufficient supplies to restock the medical clinic," Darius said, thinking of the inventory.

"The clinic's a pile of rubble," Hannah pointed out.

"We will soon have supplies to rebuild the clinic too." After interstellar communications were established, New Eden might be able to lure a doctor or two to the planet, as well. "We also have some medical training. We can keep things running until we have staff."

Hannah's eyes became shiny at that bit of news. Even though Darius knew they were happy tears, the sight tugged at him all the same. While he and his cyborg brethren had experienced a mostly sterile life in their current iterations, they had been safe. They'd had the means to defend themselves, treat their medical issues, and even terraform an asteroid again if they really needed to. New Eden had almost nothing compared to them, every available resource tapped out from overuse, new resources unreachable due to the lack of tech. Darius had vague memories of some of his previous clones and knew some of them had suffered deeply, but he hadn't. Not the new, mostly human Darius.

He turned to Rhys. "Have we woken up the rest of the settlement?"

"I'm certain some of them will be up and about soon enough." His expression darkened. "Hannah was very worried about Jasmine. She didn't know you would take her on this mission."

Darius held up his hands in defense. "I didn't, either. That was Jasmine's doing. She ran after Simon and insisted on coming along based on a promise he made to her a while back."

Rhys tilted his head. "Simon?"

Darius remembered that Simon had chosen a name while aboard the ship. "SP29."

"I assumed. I didn't know he'd renamed himself."

"I think there were a few names in the running." Speaking of Simon, Darius sneaked a glance at him speaking with the other cyborgs who'd joined them on their trip. The starboard cargo bay door yawed open, revealing stacks of crates filled with supplies. Somewhere in there were Jasmine's packages of books and fabric, paper and pencils.

Rhys didn't reply, instead scrutinizing Darius, as if he thought he was hiding something. Technically, Darius was, but it was only temporary. He kept his broadcast link closed, not wanting to give away anything before Simon and Jasmine wanted him to. If they'd okay it, Darius would happily crow from the New Eden rooftops about the new relationship.

"I see," Rhys said after an uncomfortable pause. "Most of the other cyborgs are still resting. I'll rouse them to help with the unloading."

"Don't bother them yet. We can take care of this for now. They can make the next supply run." From the corner of his eye, he spotted Jasmine and Hannah walking away, their conversation in whispers. Try as he might, his cybernetic hearing couldn't pick up their words.

"Darius."

He snapped back to attention. Rhys still wore a suspicious expression. "Sorry, I was woolgathering."

"We have work to do." Rhys nodded his head at the cargo bay. "Let's start."

"On it." Darius locked eyes with Simon, who had a massive box of construction material in his hands. He thought he actually saw Simon blush.

Just wait until we're alone again, with Jasmine, he said to him over their link.

Simon replied, *That's what's keeping me going this morning.*

Darius smiled. The work ahead would be worth it.

———

HANNAH KEPT YAWNING as she and Jasmine walked back to her house. "Go back to bed," Jasmine said.

"No way. I want to hear all about your trip to space. You're the first of us to do that since the original settlers arrived. I want to hear everything." Hannah pointed to her front door. "Go in. I'll make tea."

Jasmine had to keep herself from making a face at the thought of the New Eden dandelion tea. "We brought coffee and seeds to grow our own from the waystation."

"Really? Did you get to taste it?"

"Yes, and it was incredible." She followed Hannah into her house, a cozy space that had largely escaped the earthquake unscathed. Some of the windows were missing glass, replaced with old boards from a collapsed barn. It would be a matter of days before they could be fully repaired, Jasmine thought happily, along with so much more.

It wasn't until Hannah closed the door behind them that she asked, "What happened?"

They knew each other too well for Jasmine to deny anything. "How could you tell?"

They walked into the kitchen and Hannah turned on a lamp. "I just can." She set her battered old kettle to boil with one of the batteries the cyborgs brought them. Like Jasmine's house, Hannah's was powered by a combination of the batteries and hydroelectricity generated by the repaired power station. It was patchy in some areas of New Eden. Jasmine didn't care, as long as it worked.

Jasmine sat at the small wooden table, its top scarred from decades of use. She'd always imagined what it would be like to talk about her love life with her best friend and never thought that would happen. Now that it had, she found that she was shy about it. "Um."

Hannah's eyes widened. "Tell me."

"Okay, but don't ask me to get into specifics." She took a deep breath. "I had sex with Simon."

It took a couple of seconds for the news to register. "You mean SP29?"

Jasmine nodded. "That's his new name."

"That's good, isn't it? Didn't you want that to happen?"

"Darius was with us too."

Hannah dropped her can of dandelion leaves. "Like, in the room?"

"Well, he was part of the action." She felt herself blush.

Hannah stared at her for a few seconds, shocked into silence. She opened her mouth, as if to ask a question, then looked away. She pursed her lips together, expression unreadable, before turning her gaze back to Jasmine, still visibly shocked.

"I don't know what we are," Jasmine said. "Please don't make a big deal about this or tell anyone yet."

Hannah blinked. "Who the hell would I tell?"

"Rhys?"

"Besides him, and Rhys is a vault. He won't say anything if I ask him not to."

"Thank you for not lying too much about how you would never repeat that to a living soul."

Hannah shrugged and bent down to pick up the can of tea leaves. "We're a couple. We tell each other things. So, you had sex with Simon and Darius?"

"Darius was involved, but we didn't actually . . .you know. I don't want to go into the details. It was fun for all of us."

"I don't need the details. I'm just really surprised, is all. Are you happy?" she asked. The kettle rattled on its battery as the water boiled. She poured it over tea leaves in a pair of mismatched cups. As much as Jasmine liked the alternatives she had on the waystation, dandelion tea still smelled like home.

"Yeah. What about you?"

Hannah looked away, a small smile on her face. "Very."

"So am I, whatever we are."

"Throuple?"

Jasmine shrugged. "Why not?"

"I can hardly wait to see the three of you walking around town, holding hands. Ollie will lose his shit."

Jasmine thought about New Eden's oldest resident. He wasn't even that old, maybe in his sixties, but he had nothing good to say about anything, opposed all attempts to rebuild New Eden, and had protested against the cyborgs joining them. He was the last holdover from the old days, believing that any kind of technological advance needed to be avoided. "All Ollie has to do to make himself angry is look at the power station."

A knock at the front door interrupted them. "I bet that's Ollie right now, although he's usually considerate enough to wait until the suns have come up," said Hannah tiredly. She rose and answered the door.

To both of their pleasant surprise, it was Rodelle Lansing. The widow of New Eden's elected leader, Rodelle was the other member of their small circle. She'd withdrawn into herself since the quake and only recently started leaving her home again. So had Hannah, but she had thrown herself into working around the clock as a means of coping. Jasmine had missed both of them.

Rodelle's expression was happy and excited, the first time Jasmine had seen her this way in years. "How was the trip? Tell me everything!" Rodelle said.

Jasmine caught Hannah's eye. "Do you want some tea first?" Jasmine asked, stalling. Her voice came out louder than she'd intended. "The water's still hot."

Rodelle narrowed her eyes at Jasmine, her suspicion palpable. "What happened?"

Jasmine sighed, then exchanged a glance with Hannah. Her secret was about to have one more person in the know. "Damn it," she muttered.

"You might want something a little stiffer after hearing about Jasmine's trip," said Hannah.

Rodelle blinked in surprise and confusion. "It's a little early for wine, isn't it?" Like the tea, New Eden wine was fermented from dandelions.

"I'm not so sure about that," Hannah replied. She poured a cup of tea for Rodelle.

"I guess that makes two people you're going to tell," Jasmine said to Hannah pointedly.

"Oh, no. I think you're going to tell her. You can't keep this from Rodelle." Hannah bit her lip to keep from giggling. "I never realized how bad you are at keeping secrets. Your face shows everything you're thinking."

"Are you calling me simple?"

"No, I'm calling you an open book."

Jasmine heaved a dramatic sigh. "Ugh, fine."

"What's happened?" Rodelle looked at each of them in turn. "Brandon woke me up this morning to tell me the ship returned. He said the supply run was successful. Did something go wrong that he isn't telling me?"

Brandon lived in the house Rodelle had shared with her late husband, while Rodelle stayed in the backyard guesthouse, which was more of a glorified shed. Hannah and Jasmine had played in it when they were small and Rodelle was their babysitter. She hadn't been able to bring herself to stay in her house since her husband had died.

Jasmine wasn't sure if Brandon had noticed anything between her, Simon, and Darius. If he had, he'd been discreet. "Promise you won't tell anyone," she said.

Rodelle made a cross motion over her heart, like they were still kids. "Of course."

"I kind of had a thing with SP29—Simon—and Darius on the ship."

Rodelle's reaction wasn't as dramatic as Hannah's, but she was still clearly surprised. "Oh. Well, that's novel, I suppose."

"I don't know what we are yet. I think we're in a relationship, but I'm not sure."

"SP29's already living with you," Rodelle said.

Jasmine wondered if Darius would move in too. She hoped so. Would that count as moving too fast? Did such a thing exist in their cultures, strange as they were? "I guess we'll take this one step at a time."

"Is there any other way?" Rodelle asked.

"Beats the hell out of me. I've never had a boyfriend before, let alone two."

Rodelle regarded her with admiration. "Is it weird to say I'm proud of you?"

"Probably, but I'll take it as a compliment."

"It's not your sex life. It's that you three seem to have

found something that works for you. Finding affection or love is very difficult. Take it when you can."

Jasmine wasn't sure where she stood on the love part of her feelings yet, although she suspected she was halfway there with both of them. Affection, certainly. But it was the undercurrent of sadness in Rodelle's voice that caught her attention. "You had that with Jackson," she said, thinking of her friend's late husband. "You were the only person of our generation who found love."

A shadow crossed over Rodelle's features. "Not exactly." As if she realized she'd said too much, she looked away.

"What?" said Hannah. "Jackson adored you."

"He didn't." Rodelle's voice was uncharacteristically sharp. Hannah jumped a little in her chair at the vehemence in it. Immediately, Rodelle softened. "Look, I've never told you or anyone the truth about our marriage. It wasn't a good one. It wasn't one I would have entered into if I'd had more of a choice about the matter."

She'd grieved for years over Jackson. She'd spent months in bed, only coming out after the cyborgs arrived. When Jackson died in the quake, a big part of Rodelle had died too.

Hadn't it?

Jasmine felt unmoored at that news. "Do you want to talk about it?" she asked.

Rodelle shook her head. "Maybe someday, but for now, I want to keep that between the three of us. I didn't miss Jackson when he died." She paused, unsure how to continue. "I guess I mourned for the death of New Eden itself after the quake, not him."

"Holy shit," said Hannah softly.

"If you can find something good with two people, do

it," Rodelle urged Jasmine. To Hannah, she said, "If you've found that with Rhys, keep it."

Hannah's lower lip wobbled for a few seconds. She was probably thinking about Rhys's emergency brain surgery. He'd nearly had to be cloned again, and she would have lost him forever. She recollected her composure, and when she spoke, her voice was steady. "I never thought I'd get that. I didn't even let myself dream about it."

"We can now," Rodelle said. "Brandon said interstellar comms are on the way."

Jasmine stood. "I don't think it's too early to drink to that. Is the wine where it usually is?"

———

JASMINE'S little house was exactly as Simon remembered it. The threadbare bedding on the couch was neatly folded, just as he'd left it before they took their trip. He left Jasmine's packages in the middle of the small living room, unsure where she would want them. Darius did the same with the ones in his arms.

Darius looked around the space. "I like it."

"It needs to be reinforced." Better yet, the house should be torn down and rebuilt. Jasmine's house wasn't one that would stand up to more seismic activity. He hadn't brought up the subject with her yet, knowing it would be a sore spot. She had grown up here. Old holographs and charcoal drawings of her family—parents, grandparents, aunts, and uncles through the decades—lined the walls. Their trinkets still filled the shelves.

"We could build a new house together," Darius said, echoing his thoughts.

"I'm not sure she would go for that yet."

"What about you? Would you go for that?" Darius

pinned him with a heated stare that made Simon want to squirm in place.

"I think you know I would." He could see it now. A big, airy space. Bed big enough for three. A fully stocked kitchen with a replicator and proper water taps. A large bathtub like the ones from the old world . . .

"Do you feel that?" Darius's sharp tone pulled Simon out of his thoughts.

"Feel what?" Even as he said the words, Simon felt a low rumble deep beneath his feet. It wouldn't have been perceptible to anyone who wasn't enhanced. "Is that another ship breaking atmosphere somewhere else on the planet?" New Eden only had one landmass, the southern part of it occupied, thanks to its arable land and water supply. The northern part of the planet was completely uninhabited.

"No. Fuck me, I think it's an earthquake."

CHAPTER NINE

THE WALLS SHOOK, old holos of Hannah's great-great grandparents falling to the floor. Jasmine looked at the spots where they had been arranged, her brain unable to reconcile what was happening. "Not again!" she cried. She looked at Hannah and Rodelle in panic, seeing her terror reflected in their faces.

She couldn't move, couldn't force herself to get up from her seat at Hannah's table. It wasn't until Rodelle rose and grabbed her that her feet finally cooperated, but she couldn't understand why Rodelle was doing that. Where could they go, when the entire planet was quaking again?

Pressing both hands into her eyes, she collapsed back into her chair. She didn't want to go through the motions after another earthquake, try to rebuild from nothing . . .

A sob escaped her when she realized the shaking had stopped. Rodelle and Hannah exchanged worried glances, as if they expected the tremors to start again. "I think it's over," Hannah said cautiously. She picked up the holos and examined them before putting them back in their places on the wall.

Rhys threw open the front door. "Are you all right?"

"Yeah, I think so," said Hannah. She blinked back tears. Rhys wrapped an arm around her and planted a kiss on the top of her head. "What the hell was that?"

"Only a tremor, but it was made more dangerous than necessary by these structures. They have to be rebuilt."

"Reinforced?" asked Hannah, looking around her childhood home. Jasmine felt her heart lurch when she thought of her own house. It was in far worse shape than Hannah's.

"I'm not sure that's possible," said Rhys sadly.

The door opened again, this time revealing Simon and Darius. Heedless of the others around them, Jasmine threw herself into Simon's arms, the closest person to her. Darius wrapped his around them both. "Are you okay?" she asked.

"We're fine," said Simon. "We waited until the tremor stopped before coming over."

"How's the house?"

"Still standing for now."

Her heart sank, even though she'd known the house would have to be replaced, eventually.

"The comm tower and medical clinic are still priorities, but we have to consider rebuilding residential homes as soon as possible," Rhys announced.

Hannah sighed. "Sounds like we'll have to have another meeting at the amphitheater."

"Are you expecting much opposition to safer dwellings?" Rhys asked incredulously.

"Of course. People want to keep their homes."

"They can create new homes out of safer structures," Rhys replied, confused.

"Unenhanced people are attached to the unsafe ones."

"That's completely illogical."

Hannah sighed again. "Of course it is. People without computer processors in their brains tend to be illogical."

"Another supply run will have to be made," Darius said. "We have construction materials, but considering the circumstances and the obvious time sensitivity of this, acquiring pre-fab houses may be the most efficient way to rebuild."

Rhys nodded. "Agreed. They'll have to be constructed with shock absorbers in the foundation."

"That sounds like it'll take a long time," Hannah said.

Rhys gave a small shrug. "A few hours per house, perhaps."

"Huh. I should've figured it would be efficient." Hannah rubbed her temples. "I'll call a meeting later today at the amphitheater. When can the next crew go out?"

"I'll solicit a few volunteers and send them out this afternoon. They'll have to go farther afield to reach a station that has pre-fab structures available."

"Not it," muttered Simon.

"Me, neither," echoed Darius.

"I guess that means I'm staying too," said Jasmine.

Rhys had an unreadable look on his face. He turned to Hannah, who gave him a knowing look. It was their own silent language. Rhys gave the barest of nods to her.

"Is it safe to go back to my house?" Jasmine asked in a small voice.

"Technically, no," said Simon gently.

"Do you think there will be another earthquake?" she asked.

"I can't say for sure. It may be time to consider moving to one of the empty houses on the west end of the settlement."

"They aren't stable, either," Jasmine replied. "That's why some of the cyborgs had to stay with residents."

"Rhys took a look at them while you were gone," Hannah replied. "There's one that can be used temporarily."

Jasmine thought about the empty houses that had survived the first devastating earthquake. Abandoned for years since their inhabitants died off—from old age, from diseases that were probably preventable in every other civilized part of the galaxy, in accidents. Many of them had fallen apart from disuse or been mined for their materials for reuse. They gave Jasmine the creeps. But if what Simon said was true, they were the least-dangerous places to live in until quake-proof houses could be built.

"Let's go there," Jasmine said sadly.

"We'll help you move your things," Darius offered.

"Thank you."

Once in her house, Jasmine made a methodical sweep from room to room, picking out irreplaceable items to add to her mother's old straw bag. "Do you think we could come back for everything else?" she asked, looking at the kitchen cabinet with dismay. The dishes inside were original stock, brought to New Eden by her however-many great grandparents. She hated to leave them behind.

"Of course." Darius set aside the box he was holding. He wrapped his arms around her from behind as she looked at the cabinet, filled with her family's memories.

Jasmine picked up one of the plates and examined it under the dull, battery-powered kitchen light. The dishes were brightly patterned with rainbow stripes. "At least they haven't broken through the years."

Darius took it from her hand. "It's melamine."

The term meant nothing to Jasmine.

"Old world plastic. I'm surprised the original settlers

would use something like this, considering their beliefs," Darius replied. He put the dish back in the cabinet.

"What else would they have used?"

"Glass, maybe? Wood or another natural material? The stories I've heard about the original New Edeners give the impression that they valued them."

"We have things made of glass and wood too. They had to use jet fuel or whatever to get here," Jasmine pointed out. She extricated herself from Darius's arms to gather the dishes. "I'll need something to eat off of, anyway," she explained.

Dawn was rising when they left her house, laden with stuff. New Eden's twin suns hovered on the horizon, one a little higher than the other. It was going to be another hot and humid day, Jasmine noted with a sigh.

They moved her things on an anti-gravity pallet from the cyborgs' ship. It provided a welcome distraction to Jasmine, who hadn't seen one before. She had to keep herself from chasing after it as it zipped along to its programmed destination, a sturdy, two-story old house that was once home to the Millmans. Jasmine vaguely remembered them, an elderly, white-haired couple who had died when she was four or five years old. None of their children had survived infancy, she recalled.

As she walked through the ruined streets, Darius and Simon on either side of her, wistfulness filled her. She'd hardly dared to allow herself to daydream about having kids of her own. No one on New Eden did. Was that a possibility now? "I have a weird question," she announced.

"Sure," Simon replied.

"I probably should have asked this before, but can you . . . are either of you fertile? How does that work?"

"I can't," Darius immediately answered. "Although I'm sure it could be reversed. My original had a sterilization surgery, and that alteration was included in my DNA blue-print when I was cloned."

"Same here," Simon added.

"Oh."

"Are you thinking about children already?" Darius asked, alarmed.

"Not really. Maybe someday, but this isn't exactly an ideal time to start a family, you know? I'm also not sure if I can have kids, either." She, along with everyone else on New Eden, had suffered from nutritional deficiencies. She knew she needed to gain some weight too.

You've also had sex exactly one time. You're definitely getting way *ahead of yourself here.* She had no idea if she even wanted children someday. Before the cyborgs' arrival, the idea had been so preposterous that she never bothered entertaining it.

The Millmans' old house was a wooden and brick structure, its windows boarded over. Its yard was over-grown, a tangle of bushes and wildflowers native to New Eden. A fruit tree that had never successfully grown edible food stood sentry in the yard. Jasmine thought it could serve as a metaphor for New Eden and the original settlers' disastrous plan.

She'd forgotten that this was the street Ollie lived on until he slammed open his front door. "Did you feel that?" he bellowed.

She sighed. She guessed Ollie was about to become her problem, since she now lived closer to him than Hannah. "I did. That's why I'm here. My house isn't sound." She unlatched the house's door and pushed it open.

"That's the Millmans' house!"

"It's mine now," she snapped over her shoulder, step-ping into the darkness, Simon and Darius at her heels.

It smelled dusty inside, but at least Jasmine couldn't

detect anything rotting. Unfortunately, she couldn't see a thing, either. "Do either of you have a flashlight?" she asked. When she looked at them, she saw brightly glowing eyes. "Whoa."

"Night vision," Simon replied.

"Yeah, I got that. It's still freaky to see." She ducked back outside to the anti-grav pallet that hovered beside the house. She poked through the stuff spread on it until she found one of the cyborgs' light cubes. Once back in the house, she turned it on to survey her new home.

"This isn't horrible," Darius said, echoing her thoughts.

"It isn't." The house had been stripped of its useful contents—its dishes had been pilfered, curtains stripped to reuse the material, the furniture largely plundered. It needed to be aired out. "It's livable."

"We can get the water and power running today," Simon promised.

"We can probably get the rest of your things moved too," said Darius.

"Will you stay with me?" she asked.

Two pairs of glowing eyes blinked. An awful feeling lodged itself in the pit of her stomach. Had she made a mistake in asking about children? Had she made another asking them to stay with her?

"Yes, of course, if you want us to," Simon replied. "I was worried that you might want me off your couch."

"I do want you off my couch. I'd rather you stay in my bed," she said.

Both of them looked relieved, and she thought about their fears of revealing their relationship to their crew. She didn't want them to have to worry about that on New Eden. Theirs was an unconventional arrangement, at least here, but Jasmine was determined to make it work.

"You need a bigger one," Darius said.

"How do you know how big my bed is?"

"If it's like the rest of them on this planet, it's too small."

She smiled in the darkness. "Let's explore upstairs."

"We'll pick out a bedroom?" Simon asked as she led them to the stairs. Her light bounced off the walls.

"I'm pretty sure there's only one, maybe two, so there won't be much to choose from." Jasmine carefully ascended the stairs, Darius and Simon following, the old floorboards creaking under their feet.

"And then we'll break it in?" Darius asked in that low voice that always made her knees weak.

A bolt of heat shot through her. She grinned. "Well, yeah. We have to make it feel like it's our home."

CHAPTER TEN

THE GROUND RUMBLED beneath his boots as the ship took off again, but Simon didn't look up from his work on the comms tower to watch the launch. Spools of cables wound around the cracked floor, along with pieces of antiquated equipment he'd torn out to make way for replacements. As much as Simon wished they'd brought pre-fab structures back with them on their first supply run, he was glad they had decided to completely refit the comms tower. Almost nothing here was salvageable. Besides that, the nearest waystation hadn't had the structures they needed.

He remembered the SOS they'd received that brought them to New Eden in the first place. Hannah's voice had been preternaturally calm, as if she'd tried repeatedly to keep herself from falling into hysterics before she could finish her message. She'd told Rhys later that she had spent days combing through the comms tower, trying to put together enough equipment to get out the planet's distress call to someone, *anyone* in the galaxy. The only reason the cyborgs picked it up was because their ship had been outfitted to read almost all comm streams in the known universe. It was probably a safety feature their earlier iterations installed, in case anyone came searching for them.

Simon used to worry about that—whether there was a group out there who held a grudge against them. Their originals had been terrible people, willingly going along with unspeakable acts in the name of a shadowy corporate entity none of them could remember. They had rebelled, with their protest led by the original Rhys Hammond, and were executed for it.

A shudder ripped down Simon's spine. He refused to dredge up those memories. He didn't want to be tormented by them the way Rhys had been before his emergency brain surgery.

He pulled out a cracked console from the wall, tossing the broken pieces to the floor. The hole it left revealed a mess of wires and couplers, many of which were still usable, according to his scans. "That's a pleasant surprise," he murmured to himself.

"You're not connected to the link. What's a pleasant surprise?" Rhys asked. He hauled out an old chunk of concrete to make way for a new command center. It crumbled into dust in his hands. He sighed and brushed them off on his trousers.

"Some of the interior wiring is salvageable," Simon said, nodding to the mess in the wall. "We can splice in the new ones."

Rhys looked at the hole in the wall, then put his gloved hands over the wires, analyzing them. His eyes widened in surprise. "I'll be damned."

Simon grinned at the epithet.

"I suppose the earlier settlers never thought to destroy the interiors, just what they could see," Rhys continued.

"I wonder why they had a comms tower at all, when they were so opposed to technology. They poured concrete for it and everything." Simon thought about the old melamine dishes in Jasmine's house. "Do you think we could find old logs, see what they were using the comms tower for in the first place? It seems odd they would have one and a launchpad when they were determined to keep themselves cut off from the rest of the galaxy. I could see them establishing a temporary one as they brought in settlers and supplies, but this looks to be permanent, you know? Like it was always supposed to be here."

"That's a good idea." Rhys cast a critical eye at the pile of electronics in the middle of the floor. "I've talked about this with Hannah, and I think she's as curious about the New Eden settlers' true motivations as we are about our originals. She thinks she was able to repair the comms unit too quickly for someone who grew up without the tech, despite my reassuring her that she's smart enough to do so."

"I'm not curious about our origins," Simon said hurriedly.

Rhys regarded him thoughtfully for a few seconds. Simon tried not to fidget under his scrutiny. He didn't have to be connected to Rhys to know he was thinking about Simon's original, who had been instrumental in their revolt. Finally, he asked, "You don't want to learn more about ourselves?"

"I know myself very well. I don't care to know who Samuel Pelletier was." His original's name, one that Simon refused to use for his own. He was not another version of Samuel. Simon was his own person, grown in the ship's cloning tank some twenty-odd years ago. Like the others, he'd never cared about his exact age, though he thought Jasmine might want to commemorate events like birthdays. "I've tried not to think too much about Samuel since your . . ." He fumbled for the least insensitive word. "Incident."

"My cybernetics failure? You don't have to sugarcoat it. I nearly died." Rhys spoke the words matter-of-factly, as if he wasn't bothered by his nearly dying. "Look, I'm not going to order you to do something you don't want to, but I encourage you to reconsider your stance on researching who we are. I think this is a good opportunity for New Eden and our brethren to establish why we exist as we do."

Simon looked at the couplers in his hands, ready to be spliced into place. He peered at the network of cables in the wall. That work hadn't been done by someone unfamiliar with technology. "I don't think the original New Edeners were as anti-tech as we've been told," he mused.

Rhys looked at the hole in the wall and shrugged. "I would have to analyze the hardware to be certain. This looks like standard comms tech dating back at least two centuries."

"Look at it," Simon insisted, shaking a piece of cable. "Look at the installation methods. This was exceptionally well done. It's a permanent installation. This isn't the half-assed work of people who didn't know what they were doing. This was supposed to be a hub for interstellar comms. Look at this." He gestured at the pile of wires. "Everything's been protected against humidity. You can feel the anti-corrosive coatings. They're still intact, because they were designed to withstand the New Eden heat."

Rhys went still, contemplating Simon's words, then reached into the wall. He pulled out a chunk of cable. "Perhaps this explains why Hannah was able to get out that SOS with minimal reconstruction. The damage was only superficial."

"That explanation makes the most sense." More questions swirled around Simon's mind. "Maybe that's why the north part of the landmass is off-limits. There could be more evidence of what the original New Edeners were up to."

"The northern part is uninhabitable, and none of our scans picked up evidence of a settlement."

"We weren't looking that hard. What did the environmental report state before we made contact? I didn't record it on my internal comp."

Rhys went silent for a few minutes, eyes blanking as he accessed those details. "Some of the data is corrupted from my surgery. I can see that the northern part is rocky, its soil poor and unsuited to growing crops. There may be an extensive cave system close to its shore, but I cannot be certain. I'm unsure if we bothered to look into it after we established where the settlement was."

Caves. "God," said Simon, leaning against a solid part of the wall. It buckled under his weight, and he quickly moved away. "Do you suppose the first settlers kept things there?"

"Do you mean like pirates would?"

An odd excitement thrummed through Simon at the possibility. "Why not? A bunch of ne'er-do-wells get together, find the perfect planet to hide out. Then, when the operation falls apart, they tell their families or their descendants, whoever, that they came here to escape the terrible horrors of modern medicine and space travel."

Rhys stared at him, the expression on his face as close to aghast as Simon could imagine it. "Huh."

"When was the last time we had a mystery to solve?" Simon continued excitedly.

"You *do* realize that we're still unsure of our own origins?" Rhys deadpanned.

Simon sighed. They had recently discovered that their originals lived and died hundreds of years ago, a shock to all of them. "I meant a mystery that didn't involve intense introspection into the reasons for my own existence. I'm not prepared to think about that."

Rhys looked like he was about to speak, probably to remind Simon of their cloning way of life, thought better of it, and nodded instead. Simon bit back a grin, despite himself. His friend's newfound discretion had to be due to Hannah's influence.

Simon steered the conversation away from possible meanings of life. "A trip to the northern part is an idea worth considering. I don't remember our scans picking up significant seismic activity in that part of the planet. At some point, we may have to consider moving the settlement north, if earthquakes and tremors persist."

"Quake-proof structures are on the way. We will also install seismic activity monitors," Rhys replied.

"What if they get worse? New Eden has always had to make do with slap-dash, half-assed solutions that work only in the short term. They could have a chance to make a real new start if we see what's in the north." Simon's mind raced with possibilities. "Or we could eventually build a second settlement there. The tech exists now to make bad soil arable. We terraformed an asteroid. We can create livable land on a planet with abundant fresh water and air."

Rhys scrutinized him for a few seconds, expression unreadable. In that instant, Simon hated being disconnected from their link. "You have grand visions for New Eden's future," he finally said.

"I like to keep an open mind. What if we established a university? Large-scale trade?"

"I'm unsure if that's a possibility, given New Eden's remoteness, but I concur. Let's keep an open mind." Rhys nodded at a brand new auxiliary command unit waiting on the floor. "Now, let's get that installed."

DARIUS STARED at the floor where the couch once rested, shocked into uncharacteristic silence. There was now a couch-shaped hole in the floorboards where it had fallen through, ringed with splinters.

Jasmine spoke first. "Fuck."

He was inclined to agree. "Do you believe us now when we say you have to leave this house?"

"I did before, but I wasn't expecting to have that point hammered home like this." She took a couple of cautious steps toward the couch. Darius grabbed her arm to keep her from moving forward.

"Don't," he said. "Let me take care of this. I won't get hurt if I fall through the floor."

She gave him a withering look. "Neither will I. I'll sink about ten centimeters to the ground. Hardly a lethal height."

"And what will you do when the entire house falls down around your ears? I can dig myself out of a house collapse without worrying about a concussion or worse."

She sighed. He had her there. "And then I'd be the next New Edener to die from a stupid accident. You're right."

"The important things are already in your new house. We'll get the furniture moved next. From now on, consider this place officially condemned. Don't come back inside."

Sadness crossed her features, and he felt like kicking himself at his flippant words. When he spoke again, his voice was softer. Kinder. "How long did your family live here?"

"My great-great-grandparents built this place, so over a hundred years. I'm not sure. Maybe longer." She looked at the walls, now bare of the holographs that chronicled generations of Sinclairs. "They came here with the first group of settlers. And now I'm the last one."

Darius knew that Jasmine had experienced tremendous loss, as had everyone on New Eden. But she hid her grief and loneliness behind an extroverted exterior in a way the other New Edeners didn't. It was one of the reasons he and Simon had been so attracted to her in the beginning. She'd radiated hope and optimism to their brethren, shown them that it was okay to be happy. Guilt pulled at Darius when he realized a huge part of that had been an act for their benefit, or a coping mechanism. Like how Hannah's was to throw herself into work around the clock.

"You're not alone anymore," he said.

She turned shining eyes to him. "I wasn't before." She paused. "Sorry, that came out wrong. I mean, I wasn't before. I have friends. But Rodelle and Hannah haven't been the same since the earthquake. Rodelle's husband and Hannah's parents died in it. My parents passed years ago. I've had a long time to get used to them being gone. I had to wait for them to catch up in their grief, you know?"

Darius didn't, not knowing anyone who had died while in this current iteration.

A flash of an unfamiliar memory assailed his senses: Simon collapsing, a crimson stain spreading across his shirt, Darius catching him, raw grief eclipsed by rage. The image was brief, but so intense, that he nearly fell against the wall.

Goddamn it, is my brain's comp failing like Rhys's?

Just as quickly, it was gone. He straightened and hoped that Jasmine didn't notice, to no avail. "Are you okay?" she asked.

He hesitated, considering what to tell her, then sighed, knowing how she would react once he gave her the truth. "I had a flashback."

"What?" Her eyes widened. No doubt, she was thinking of Rhys.

He tried to reassure her. "Everyone gets them from time to time. This won't be like Rhys's situation, I promise. He was having them all the time, and he had faulty tech in his head. Mine is standard."

She looked unconvinced. "Are you sure?"

"Yes."

She paused. "What was it about?"

"I saw Simon die. I think he was shot."

She gasped. In the dim light offered by the battery-powered illuminators, he thought he saw her eyes fill with tears. "Why?"

"I don't know. I know it wasn't related to our originals' deaths by execution, so it must have been an earlier cyborg iteration. I'm not sure I *want* to know."

"Were you two involved before?"

Darius thought about the image of Simon falling against him. Then he remembered how he'd always felt a special affection for him, how it had evolved into physical attraction to what he had now, which he didn't have a name for. "I think so, but I don't know for sure. It's more of a gut feeling, you know?"

She nodded. "Can I ask you something else about you two?"

"Shoot."

"How long were you two a couple before I came along?"

"We weren't. Shortly before our asteroid was destroyed, we had a night together at a deep space station hotel during a supply run. That was it, until our time together on the ship." Just the mention of the three of them in her cabin was enough to set his body temperature soaring, his cock stiffening. He could hardly wait to do it again.

Jasmine blushed. "Oh."

Darius put a finger under her chin and tilted it up, pinning her with a stare. "That was incredible, by the way."

"I worried about that, you know. That I wasn't better."

"Neither of us cared about that, and it isn't as though we have much to compare it to. Watching Simon fuck you was one of the hottest things I've ever seen." He dropped his hand to her shoulder, then slid it down her back to squeeze her ass. "Of course, I'm hoping to get a chance to do that myself."

Her breath caught. "You weren't jealous?"

"As long as it's only me or Simon inside you, not at all." He took a half-step closer to her, so he could press his erection against her hip. "Or both of us."

She gasped, then leaned into him, and he grinned at the sensation. The small amount of friction drove him crazy, and if they hadn't been standing in a house on the verge of collapse, he would have pinned her against the wall already. The sensors in his hands reported that her heart rate increased, his skin heating against his touch. She wanted this as much as he did. He hated having to wait.

Jasmine twined her arms around his neck and placed a feathery kiss on his lips, a gesture that was almost chaste. He bit back a moan. When she spoke, the raspy note in her voice belied it. "You'll have to tell me about your night with Simon sometime. I want to know what he likes."

He nipped the tender spot under her ear, remembering how Simon liked that too. "I'll show you."

CHAPTER ELEVEN

The twin suns were high in the sky by late morning. Darius had left Jasmine's house to help a couple of neighbors move out, and she was acutely aware of his absence. The anti-grav pallet sped alongside Jasmine as she walked back to her new home, packed with the remains of her kitchen. There wasn't much—eggs, a few jars of vegetables she and Hannah had carefully preserved, a cloudy glass jar that held a few dregs of flour milled before the quake, and a couple bottles of dandelion wine. Resentment welled in her as she plodded along. Despite the brief, pleasurable exchange she'd had with Darius, she didn't want to move. She didn't want to leave her home, the last remnant of her life with her family, didn't want to surrender even more to New Eden's geologic whims.

Quick footsteps behind her had Jasmine stopping in her tracks and turning around. "Hannah?"

"We're having a meeting this afternoon at the amphitheater," she said briskly, hardly out of breath after her run.

Uncharacteristic irritation swept over her. "Another one?"

"This is important."

"They're always important. Couldn't you make an executive decision?" Jasmine rubbed her temples. "Sorry, I don't mean to be a bitch. I just want to move my shit over to my new house and start my life over, yet again."

"You're not being one, and I get it." Hannah's voice dropped, even though there wasn't another soul around them who could hear. "Rhys and Simon were putting the comms tower back together, and they don't think the original New Eden settlers were as tech-phobic as they seemed to be."

"Of course, they weren't. They took a spaceship to get here, didn't they?"

"Yeah, but they have a theory that it was all a sham. They're going to announce a trip to the northern part of the landmass to see what they could have been hiding there."

Jasmine stared at her. "Why? All that's there is a bunch of rocks."

"Their ship scanners picked up evidence of a cave network. Right now, the theory is the New Eden settlers were, I don't know, smugglers or something, who set up a settlement after the last stop to nowhere to hide out."

"That's insane."

"It is, and Simon explains it a lot better. They want to see if any New Edeners want to make the trip out there once the other cyborgs have come back with supplies."

Curiosity got the better of Jasmine. "I'd go."

"You're already the first of us to see outer space. Let someone else be the first to explore the north." Hannah smiled.

"Do you want to go?"

Her smile faded. "Fuck, no. I don't want to be the one to come across James Thierry's body. Or any of the others who might have explored the north before he wandered off. I've had enough excitement for a lifetime over the last couple of weeks. All I want to do is preserve tomatoes and spend as much time in bed with Rhys as I can. Not in that order."

"Oh, shit. I forgot about James." Jasmine clapped a hand over her mouth in horror. James had been one of the few people in their age group, and he'd wandered off to the north five years ago after his uncle and last remaining relative died, never to be heard from again. "Sorry, that came out wrong. I know you two had a history."

Hannah shrugged, expression unreadable. "It's fine. You know what this place can be like."

"Are things still going okay for you and Rhys?"

"Better than okay, although he's talking about us leaving the house too. He's doing a seismic test or something on our street. I don't know the details." She sighed. "I don't want to go, but if it's about to fall into a sinkhole, I'll have to. Hey, have you tried out the water pumps in your new place?"

"They work, but we don't have hot water yet."

"I'm sure it'll be hooked up soon." Hannah looked at the pile of stuff on the anti-grav pallet. "I'm going to the amphitheater. I'll see you there soon?"

"Unfortunately."

"It'll be quick, I think. Rhys wants everyone to be on board with an expedition and the possibility of our entire reason for existing on this fucking backwater being a lie. It's like something out of a novel." She tilted her head, as if remembering something. "You brought books back, didn't you?"

"A huge stack, all antiques. It turns out, the rest of the universe doesn't have much use for paper anymore."

"Pass a couple on to me? It would be nice to have something to entertain myself with."

"Of course." She and Darius had already moved her precious books to the house. "We'll have to build a proper library someday.".

Hannah nodded. "Pick out a couple of good ones for me. I'm going to the amphitheater. See you there?"

"Yeah." Jasmine suppressed a sigh, not wanting to appear ungrateful in front of her best friend. Hannah had done a lot for New Eden, probably more than anyone, given her unending devotion to the food supply. It wouldn't take much out of Jasmine to suck it up and endure one more community meeting, especially for something as exciting as exploring the north.

She returned to the new house, leaving her things in the kitchen. Once she was back outside, she eyed the waiting anti-grav pallet. It hovered a meter off the scrubby ground, bobbing in place. Weariness pulled at her, a reminder that she was short on sleep.

What the hell, it was worth a shot. Jasmine carefully climbed on it and lay back. "Move," she commanded it. The pallet jerked forward a few meters, then stopped. "Follow the path." It didn't obey, instead bobbing lightly in place. Then it sank, nearly reaching the ground. "Damn it." She hopped off, and it floated to its original position. With a sigh, she walked to the amphitheater instead, leaving it hovering over the path.

There was already a crowd assembled when she arrived. She spotted Rodelle and waved, taking a seat next to her. "You look exhausted," Rodelle said by way of greeting.

"I feel exhausted. Did anyone tell you what this

meeting is about?"

"Brandon said there might be something in the north about our ancestors." She was cut off by Hannah calling the meeting to order.

To Jasmine's surprise, Simon was on the dais next to her and Rhys. She leaned forward in anticipation. Simon caught her eye and gave her a smile that made her toes curl in her sandals. She thought about what he looked like in the throes of passion, then about the kiss she'd shared with Darius. Her knees went weak. Why the hell did she have to be tortured like this, looking at one of the men she was crazy about, unable to touch him?

Simon was all business when he spoke, voice brusque. "We've discovered evidence that the first settlers didn't come here because they were running away from technology."

Even though she already knew that, Jasmine still felt like the proverbial rug had been pulled out from under her. A few people asked questions, Ollie being the loudest as usual, and Simon spoke over them. "The comms tower wasn't constructed by amateurs. It was meant to be used for covert communications, and it was deliberately destroyed in a way to evade detection by intergalactic authorities. We suspect that the original settlers weren't settlers at all, but criminals who eventually set up a colony as a cover for their activities."

Silence descended over the group at that piece of information. Even though she had already been told a truncated version of that theory, Jasmine found herself speechless. It was so outlandish to consider, absolutely impossible that their however-many great-grandparents would set up a colony that was doomed to fail in a few generations, just to hide away unknown criminal proceeds.

Ollie, New Eden's resident grouch, was the first to

speak once he'd collected his thoughts. "Doesn't it make more sense that we're in this position because of their ideals? Occam's razor and whatnot?"

It was the first rational sentence the man had uttered in Jasmine's memory. Ollie, who had staunchly defended the old ways to the point of pounding on Hannah's door to complain in the wee hours of the morning. Ollie, who had been the only one to refuse to accept cyborg help in deference to the old ways. Ollie, who had initially refused to allow any of them to take up residence in the empty houses out of a bizarre power trip.

Ollie, who was now Jasmine's direct neighbor. "Goddamn it," she mumbled under her breath. She'd forgotten about that in the mad move from her childhood home. Why was he on board with the criminal theory when, just today, he had protested her moving into her new house?

"The way the comms tower was constructed and destroyed does not speak of people who didn't know what they were doing or didn't respect it," Simon insisted. "The tech used was high quality for its era. It wasn't destroyed so much as disabled. That's why Hannah was able to eventually repair it to get out the SOS that brought us here."

Jasmine's breath caught. Judging by the stunned looks on everyone's faces, she wasn't the only one who was shocked. She felt like an idiot as she thought further about the cyborgs' theory. Hannah had cobbled together a workable interstellar broadcast system from old manuals that fell apart in her hands. It had taken weeks for her to do it, working by the light of a makeshift torch late into the night, but she'd done it. Without any replacement parts, without anyone who could repair something more complex than a water pump. The comms system hadn't needed them. It had been a matter of splicing wires back together and seeing what happened.

Because the comms system hadn't been destroyed; it had merely been disabled. And it had been waiting all these years for someone to put it back together, to cry out to the universe for help.

A fresh wave of respect for Hannah and her determination rose in Jasmine. She had always loved Hannah like the sister she'd never had, admired her resourcefulness and work ethic, her refusal to lie back and wait to die like so many New Edeners had before the cyborgs arrived. Even Jasmine's upbeat and positive attitude had waned in the weeks before they'd landed in the field near the settlement; it had become an act that had become harder and harder to maintain since the earthquake.

Hannah finally spoke. "There are other clues about the real motives of the original settlers. Think about the power station. When it was first constructed, it was designed to provide way more electricity than a small settlement of Luddites could ever need. It was built that way to accommodate the comms tower and landing pad, maybe more. In its prime, it could have serviced up to thirty thousand homes. There's never been more than a couple hundred people here at a time." She didn't have to add the depressing truth about there being barely a tenth of that number left, after a decade of tremors, quakes, and illnesses.

Thirty thousand people. No, structures that would suck up the energy that could be used by thirty thousand people. Jasmine's mind reeled.

"It's been brought to our attention that there's a possibility of more clues being in the north," Hannah said.

Conversation rose again, more questions thrown at her. She held up a hand before continuing. "We all know the stories we've been told about how dangerous the northern part of the land is. But none of us have been there; our parents didn't go there. The cyborgs' comps picked up signs that there isn't just a bunch of rocks and untillable soil in the north. We'll be putting together an expedition team to explore it."

Another burst of chatter came forth, a mix of people protesting and offering to go. Curiosity welled up in Jasmine at the prospect, and with it, a sense of adventure. She'd been to space and could do with a trip to the north, despite Hannah's misgivings about such a journey. Looking around the crowd for Darius, she spotted him a few meters away, closer to the stage, and started to thread her way through the crowd toward him. She'd mentioned joining such a trip to Hannah, and her curiosity about what could be there still pulled at her. It might be even more exciting than leaving the planet.

He'd been watching Simon so intently that he started when Jasmine touched his hand. He looked at her, a smile forming on his face, before lightly squeezing her fingers in response, the ports in his rasping against her skin.

She balanced on her tiptoes to whisper in his ear. "Do you want to go to the north?"

He blinked in surprise. "Do you?"

That wasn't encouraging. "I asked you first."

He hesitated before he replied. "Simon already told me he doesn't want to go."

She felt deflated at that bit of news. She didn't want to go without both of them. "Oh."

"It'll be dangerous," he murmured in her ear. "I don't want to see either of my favorite people falling into a cave."

"How do you fall into a cave? Don't you just walk in? Now I really want to go."

"Maybe after the cave system has been explored and documented."

His breath sent tingles down her body, spiraling to her core. She felt her cheeks heat. A discussion of cave exploration should not be sexy, but damn it if Darius couldn't make it so.

"You're blushing," he said in that same voice that made her toes curl.

"You have that effect on me."

He gave a low growl in reply, meant for her ears only. Judging by the way Simon's eyes slightly widened, Darius had sent that to him too.

"Would it be inappropriate to talk about caves and exploration right now?" he asked.

"Yes. I am not a cave," she whispered.

"There are so many similes I could be making."

Her reply was a stage whisper. "Darius!"

He grinned at her, the sight forcing her into forgiving him.

Simon caught their eyes, then hopped off the stage, leaving Rhys and Hannah to argue with the others over who would make the trek to the north. "We're not going," Simon said before either of them could speak.

"I already told her," Darius said.

"This isn't fair. I should be plugged in to you two," Jasmine grumbled.

"That can definitely be arranged," Darius purred.

Simon's eyes had taken on a glazed quality that reminded her of what he looked like over her, thrusting in and out of her body. She had no doubt what he was thinking about. "Maybe tonight?" she asked quietly, mindful of the others around them. Whatever they had would be public knowledge at some point, she was sure, but she wasn't ready to talk about having two boyfriends just yet. If they were her boyfriends and not a fling. Her heart hurt to even consider that possibility.

"So, it's settled. Brandon and CW44 have volunteered to go to the north," Hannah announced.

Had they? Jasmine hadn't been paying attention.

"Anyone else who wants to go with them—let them know. If you can tolerate the trek, they'd be glad for the help," Hannah added.

"How long should it take?" Jasmine asked Simon.

"Three or four days each way. We don't have anti-grav vehicles, so whoever goes will have to walk the entire way."

While Jasmine had a taste for adventure, she wasn't sure she could handle multiple days of walking. Nor was she sure that she, Darius, and Simon would return in a timely manner if they were together and had all that privacy of the proverbial open road. "I see."

The crowd dispersed, a few stragglers hanging behind to ask about accompanying Brandon to the north. With Simon and Darius on either side of her, Jasmine began the walk back to her new house. Her heart squeezed painfully at the thought of her old one, ready to fall down if someone coughed on it.

Her house, built by her family, who may have been criminals. She sighed. Her parents had been gone for years now, but at that moment, Jasmine missed them fiercely. Both of them would have been infinitely amused at the possibility of their predecessors being smugglers. She could picture them sitting around their kitchen table, her father giving her and her mother his best impression of an old world pirate lifted from the yellowing copies of his beloved adventure novels. Books that had long ago disintegrated from age. Jasmine swallowed the lump in her throat as she thought of them.

What would they think of her boyfriend situation? Jasmine had no idea. There had been so few potential partners to choose from by the time she was born. She and

Hannah were among the youngest of New Eden's residents, with their few peers having passed away far too soon.

When she reached her new house, she paused for a moment before entering, staring at the structure. The house looked as desolate as she felt, unloved and abandoned. If Jasmine believed in ghosts, she would have thought it appeared haunted.

With a gusty sigh, she walked inside.

————

HE SHOULD HAVE BEEN THINKING about the latest development on New Eden, but Darius's hormones had taken over. His internal comp told him that Simon was nearby, descending the comms tower stairs to the basement, where Darius was currently putting the finishing touches on the foundation's repairs. Fresh sealant glowed in the three hairline cracks that had formed over the course of New Eden's tremors and quakes. He took a step back to admire his handiwork, sensing Simon approaching him from behind. He didn't turn around, instead waiting for Simon to wrap his arms around his waist and press a kiss to his cheek. "That looks great," Simon said in his ear.

A shiver of pleasure traveled through Darius at the contact. "Compared to the rest of the tower's repairs, this was the easy part." Under his enhanced suit, his skin prickled with awareness at Simon's nearness. He felt the first stirrings of arousal thrum through him, which he tamped down. They were alone in the basement, but there were others around them in the tower. Simon was shy. Plus, there was something else he wanted to mention that had nothing to do with how his hormones were misbehaving. "You're right about the comms tower and the skills that went into constructing it. This place was built to withstand earthquakes."

"We all feel like idiots for not thinking of that sooner." Simon's hold on him tightened. Darius threaded his fingers through Simon's and leaned against him, his back against Simon's chest a warm comfort. "The important thing is we're getting everything back online. The comms tower should be fully functional within the week."

"Incredible. I'm proud of you." Of course, if New Eden hadn't been kept in the dark ages for as long as it had been, the comms tower would have been up and running in a matter of hours.

"It was a group effort," Simon replied, but his protest was weak. Darius could feel his hardening erection pressing against him and knew Simon was no longer thinking about the comms tower. His internal comp told him that Simon's body temperature was rising, heartbeat increasing.

Darius grinned. "You know, we could make another group effort if we go back to Jasmine's."

Simon's head bobbed against his shoulder, body shaking with laughter. Something in Darius untwisted, a knot of worry he'd had for months about Simon's distance, his unhappiness with everything in his life. It was good to hear and feel that again. "If she'll have us," Simon said.

"Oh, she will. We already talked about that."

Just as quickly as it started, Simon's mirth evaporated. "Does it bother you that she's—well, there? I care about both of you so much." His voice caught, and he was quiet for a moment, gathering his thoughts. Darius remained still, waiting for him to continue. When he did, his voice was stronger. "I've never felt this way about anyone before. Maybe you, as an earlier clone. You've always been familiar to me, every time I woke up in the tank."

Darius's breathing stilled. "Of course, it doesn't bother

me. You and Jasmine are my favorite people in the universe." Softly, he added, "You remember all of those times?" He'd been present the last time Simon was cloned. He hadn't been out of the tank much longer than Simon had.

"Sort of, at least a couple of them. It's vague, like I wasn't there. Like I'm remembering someone telling me about their experiences, rather than my own memories. Does that make sense?"

Darius thought about his own recalled memory of Simon dying in his arms. Memory shards, Rhys sometimes called them. The term was appropriate; it felt like a shard pierced his heart every time he remembered it. But it didn't feel real, more of a horrifying theoretical situation he didn't want to think about. "Yes."

"I wonder if we were a couple before," Simon mused.

"*We* weren't. Samuel and the first Darius might have been."

Simon gave a half-shrug. "Who knows how that kind of relationship would have been tolerated in the old world? Or whatever fucked-up military complex we ended up in after agreeing to the cybernetic enhancements?"

"Maybe our originals knew one another as children. Maybe they were friends." For the first time in his memory, Darius longed to know more about their backgrounds. Their brethren had largely agreed to let the past stay there, mostly because they didn't want to draw attention to themselves to whatever lay beyond this isolated corner of the galaxy. There was very little about the cyborgs' origins aboard the ship, indicating that earlier iterations deliberately destroyed files. Unlike whoever did the same to New Eden's comms tower, it had been thorough and irreversible. Their originals and first iterations had probably been awful people. It was anyone's guess who they'd pissed off over the centuries.

"I think that's the most sentimental thing I've ever heard you say." Simon lay his head on Darius's shoulder for a moment, the embrace warm and comforting.

"Simon?"

"Mm?"

"Why were you so put off by me and Jasmine? You know no one would care about our relationship, right? We're all adults." Darius held his breath, wondering if he'd just made a huge mistake in asking Simon about that.

Simon sighed. "Would it be clichéd to say I'm bad at relationships?"

"Yes, and you don't know if you are. You've never been in one before."

"Our previous . . ."

"Dead clones don't count." He felt Simon flinch at the words but forged on. "We're not them. We've all given ourselves chances to start over a few times, and now that we're on New Eden, we can make a real attempt at living proper lives. We can have a relationship with Jasmine." He held his breath, carefully parsing his next words. "You *do* want to include her?"

"I can't imagine not being with both of you. That's part of why I was so distant before. I thought I had to choose. I didn't want to break either of your hearts. Or mine."

"You won't. And I dreamed about being with both of you. I didn't want to have to choose, either."

"Yeah, you made that pretty obvious." Simon raised his head and pressed a kiss to Darius's neck. "Let's go see her now."

Darius grinned. "How fast can you run?"

"As fast as you. I'll race you to the house, in fact."

It wasn't until they were out of the comms tower basement, standing in the waning sunshine, that they bolted for the opposite end of the settlement. They were at Jasmine's door in a matter of minutes, hardly out of breath from the exertion. She stood on the stoop, a basket of eggs held in her hand and a bewildered look on her face that Darius wanted to kiss off. "You two looked like giant blurs," she said incredulously.

Darius grinned. "We couldn't wait to see you."

She blushed, color spreading across her tanned face. "I've missed you two too," she said, pushing open the door, and they followed her inside.

Jasmine had set up a couple of lights with the cybernetic batteries, and they glowed dully against the wooden walls. She left the eggs in an icebox that hadn't been there this afternoon. After she closed it, she turned around to face them. Her face was still flushed, her pulse picking up speed. Her tongue darted out from between her lips as her gaze flickered between them. It was a small gesture, but it still sent a thrill straight through Darius. He didn't have to be connected to Simon to know he felt the same.

When she spoke again, she sounded breathless. "I don't have my bedroom set up yet."

"I'm sure we can figure something out." Darius closed the small distance between them, pressing his lips to hers as he'd wanted to do all afternoon. She gasped, her mouth quivering against his. He didn't break the kiss until Simon nudged him, and he stepped away to let him do the same to her. It reminded him of when he'd watched Simon fuck her.

Darius's breath caught, and it wasn't until his cybernetics forced the air from his lungs that he remembered to breathe again. He had to resist the urge to stroke his aching cock over his pants, now uncomfortably tight.

Jasmine looked dazed when Simon pulled away, pupils dilating in a way that Darius was coming to love. So did Simon, for that matter. Darius grinned. This was going to be fun. "I'm going to show you what Simon likes," he murmured in Jasmine's ear. To Simon, he said, "Jasmine and I started something in the old house that we should finish together."

"Seriously? That's not fair." Simon's tone was petulant, but it was put upon, forced. To Jasmine, he said, "I should tell you that Darius and I had a moment in the comms tower basement."

"Darius, what the hell?" Like Simon, Jasmine's voice held a note of amusement. "Are you just working your way across New Eden, getting everyone around you worked up and then taking off?"

"Not New Eden, just you two."

"And a gross old basement, really? Simon, you deserve better."

"It's a good thing we're in this house then, isn't it?" Before either of them could answer, Darius squeezed Jasmine's ass, drawing a squeal from her. "The living room is closest, and I couldn't help but notice it has furniture that will work for what I have in mind tonight."

"I thought having sex with us is what you have in mind," Jasmine said.

Darius looped an arm around each of their waists, drawing them to him. The ever-present readout in the corner of his vision reported their vitals, how they were responding to his presence. "Oh, it is. It's just going to be a little different today than it was on the ship. I plan on being a more active participant this time. Watching Simon fuck you was the hottest thing I've ever seen, and I've been dreaming about my chance to do that too."

The living room had been set up with an oversized,

threadbare couch that Jasmine had covered with a thin bedsheet. A matching chaise, also covered with a sheet, was arranged next to it. Letting go of Jasmine and Simon, Darius pushed the chaise in front of the couch, creating a makeshift bed. It would be a tight squeeze, but it would work for what Darius had in mind.

"I want to see that, too." Simon's voice was rough as he looked at Darius and Jasmine in turn. "We had that one night together right after we evacuated from our asteroid. It wasn't enough." The answer surprised Darius. Simon had always been so reluctant to talk about their attraction.

Something melted in Darius at that admission, and he realized that he hadn't known how much he wanted to hear Simon say those words until now. He'd felt like Simon's mistake, his secret shame, for far too long. He slid an arm around Simon and kissed him soundly, tongue tangling with his. His cock was so hard it hurt, but he ignored it for the moment, putting everything he could into kissing Simon. "Thank you," he murmured.

Simon nuzzled Darius to nip at his ear, sending a ripple of desire down Darius's spine. "I meant it," he whispered. Louder, he said, "To answer your question, Jasmine, Darius and I have fucked each other a couple of times."

A becoming blush touched her cheeks. "Oh."

Simon sank down on the couch cushions, the sheet puffing up a little around his body as he did so, his long legs stretched out. "We'll have a chance to try everything together," he promised, giving both of them knowing looks. "Jasmine, come here."

Darius already liked where this was going. He'd planned on being in charge tonight, but he wasn't averse to Simon taking the lead. Jasmine obeyed, arranging herself over his body, straddling his hips. His body bucked under her, an involuntary movement, before taking her face in his hands and kissing her. Darius settled himself behind her, a knee on either side of Darius's legs, then brushed aside her hair to kiss her neck. She let out a gasp that turned into a mewl of pleasure, back arching against Darius. He took the opportunity to grip her hips, grinding his aching erection against her ass. "I'm going to tell you what Simon likes," he said.

She turned her head to face him and nodded. "Yes."

The breathy reply made him grind his teeth in frustration that none of them were naked yet. Slipping his hand under her shirt, he felt goose bumps rise as he traced a path along her skin. He skimmed over her ribs, to the underside of her breasts, her nipples tight and hard under his touch. He pinched one, drawing another harsh gasp from her, the noise bringing a small smile to Simon's face. Darius pulled Jasmine's shirt over her head and tossed it away, not caring where it landed. "Move down a little. Give Simon some room to take off his trousers." His gaze landed on Simon, who gave Darius another smile that could melt his systems before reaching for the seal on his trousers.

Jasmine wiggled away, watching as Simon unsealed his clothes. Understanding dawned on her face when he freed his cock, stroking it a couple of times. Jasmine reached for it, eyes meeting his for permission before Simon nodded. She wrapped her hand around its base, sliding it up and down, as if getting a feel for it. Then she leaned over and licked the tip experimentally, without prompting from either of them. The sight was enough to make Darius's mouth dry. "That's exactly what Simon likes," Darius said.

She lifted her head. "Is this what you were hinting at?"

"I'd hardly call that hinting, but yes."

"I've thought about this too," Jasmine said thoughtfully. She stroked her hand along Simon's shaft again, the motion so intense that Simon threw his head against the couch cushions. She leaned down again, putting her mouth over his cock before Darius could point out that all of them had been thinking about it, all of them wanted to act on those impulses.

Simon moaned, putting his hands in her hair as her head bobbed up and down. "She's good at this," he said through gritted teeth. A happy little noise sounded from Jasmine as she sucked.

"She looks like she is. A natural." Darius unsealed his own clothing, pushing his trousers down his hips before taking his erection in hand as he watched the scene in front of him. Simon's breath came out in tortured gasps as Jasmine worked her mouth and hands over his cock, hips lifting in time to the rhythm she'd established. Darius settled behind her, taking care to avoid resting on Simon's splayed legs, then skimmed a hand over her upraised ass, lightly spanking it. A mewl of surprise escaped her throat, but she didn't stop her ministrations on Simon. Darius reached for the drawstring on her loose trousers. She paused, lifting her head from Simon's lap to look at him behind her. "Can I?" he asked.

She nodded, eyes glazed, face flushed. "Yes."

Darius peeled off her clothing. He smacked her ass again while she obediently lifted a knee, one at a time, to help him. "Simon's waiting," he said.

Jasmine bent over Simon again, lips wrapping around his cock and sucking. Darius slid a hand over her bare skin to her front, dipping a finger into the warm well of her sex, already soaked. He dragged it to her clit, rubbing in tight, slow circles until she trembled against his hand, on the verge of an orgasm. She shuddered against him, and for a half-second, he considered letting her have one.

He abruptly pulled his hand away, deciding against it.

"Not yet," he commanded.

Simon stroked his hand along her hair. "She was close," he said. "You're being rude."

"I'm not. I'm just making her wait a little longer." She raised her head. "Jasmine, now you're being rude. Simon isn't finished yet."

She bit back a pained laugh before resuming. Simon's hips bucked against her mouth, a sure sign that he was close too.

Darius wasn't content to watch this time. He urged Jasmine's legs farther apart, cock in hand, and dragged it along the wet seam of her pussy. She cried out, ass pressing against him, but didn't lift her head again. Darius pushed himself into her, slowly as he could, fighting the urge to sink all the way inside. He let out a groan at the feeling of her surrounding him as he maneuvered another inch inside her.

When Jasmine lifted her head, Simon didn't utter a word of protest. His eyes were half-lidded, glazed with lust as he watched Darius eased into her. "She feels good, doesn't she?" was all Simon said.

Darius nodded, feeling beads of sweat pop up along his brow. Fully seated inside her, he fought for control as he gave her time to adjust. It was only her second time, ever, and his first time with a woman, and it was a novelty for both of them. He could truly understand now the Herculean effort it had taken Simon not to rut her silly.

Jasmine moaned and pushed back against him, a sign that she was comfortable. Darius withdrew and surged back into her with more force than he'd intended, but she just pushed again, crying out as she did so.

That was all the encouragement Darius needed. He pounded into her, hands gripping her hips, grunts leaving him as he surged into her. Hands splayed on Simon's stomach, she lowered her face to her his cock again, greedily sucking it as Simon fisted his hands in her hair. Catching Simon's eye again, Darius said, "I'm not going to last."

He grimaced, a sure sign he was close. "Me neither."

"Fuck me, she feels good." As Darius bit out the words, Simon threw his head back, body stiffening as his orgasm crashed through him. Darius's hand slipped around Jasmine, finding her clit again as he thrust into her. He was so close himself, but a sense of abysmal selfishness crested through him when he thought about what she was doing for him, for both of them. She responded immediately, lifting her head from Simon's cock, little cries of pleasure increasing in volume as Darius stroked her clit. Her pussy began to clench around him, a sensation that sent a hit of masculine pride rippling through him. Darius gritted his teeth, holding off on his own orgasm as best he could as she rode hers on his cock. It wasn't until she exploded on him that he gave in, orgasm ripping through his body while Simon watched.

Silence descended on the room as Darius's climax subsided, the only sounds that of their labored breathing. Still inside her, Darius urged her to shift positions, so she was in his lap while he rested on his knees. Simon sat up to wrap his arms around them both, pressing heated kisses to each.

Darius had started this to scratch itches he hadn't known he'd had until he'd seen both of them. Gratefulness flowed through him that he didn't have to choose, that he could keep both for now, that he could love them together. He did, more than anything, and would do whatever he had to in order to keep them with him.

Not wanting to ruin the moment, he kept that knowledge to himself. There was plenty of time to talk of love later.

Jasmine sank into the old wooden chair's cushion, the first thing she'd made when she started working with textiles. It felt like a million years ago, although she guessed it to be ten or eleven. The cushion, stuffed with straw and bits of rags, had miraculously survived being torn apart for pillows, something she was grateful for now. She was sore in places she hadn't been before. Heat crept up her face when she remembered exactly *why* she was sore.

She missed Simon and Darius already, and they'd only parted less than an hour ago. They were working at the comms tower again, putting the finishing touches on something electric. Jasmine had zoned out during the technical part of their discussion at breakfast. Then they'd kissed her goodbye, and it had been all she could do to keep herself from asking them to skip their shifts at the tower for a few hours . . .

She shook her head, as if she could dislodge her fantasies that way, and focused on the task at hand. She was in an old tack room in the barn that had been appropriated for textile production years ago. In the corner was a long-disused loom, brought here by the original settlers, not that there were any cloth fibers left to weave. In front of her was a table, its top worn smooth with age. Its survival could also be chalked up to divine intervention over the years. An ancient sewing machine with a foot-operated treadle rested on it, surrounded by the piles of fabric Jasmine bought at the waystation. She had finally unearthed the old patterns she had stashed in a wooden box under a loose floorboard in the barn, saved against all odds that she might have use for them someday.

She took a deep breath, the air faintly scented with the fragrance of hay, contentment filling her for the first time in recent memory. She could finally create some new clothes for the residents of New Eden, the first they would have in years. Everyone had been going about in done-over pieces, frayed to their last threads, for almost as long as she could remember. Jasmine wasn't a gardener, farmer, or engineer. Her skills and interests lay in matters outside the practical; a predilection for drawing, reading novels, and sewing clothes bordered on useless on a planet like New Eden. As she placed the pattern on a piece of fabric and carefully pinned it into place, she wondered if she might actually have a chance to be useful again.

She had cut out the fabric and loaded the sewing machine with a spool of new thread when a voice called her name. Blinking, she looked up to see Hannah and Rodelle in the tack room doorway. Rodelle held a platter in her hand. "We brought breakfast," she said, face splitting into a grin.

Jasmine blinked again. When was the last time she'd seen Rodelle smile like that? "Thank you. This is unexpected." She pulled the thread through the needle. "Although I should tell you, I've already eaten breakfast."

"You haven't had these," Hannah said smugly. She

pushed a stool to the side of the table opposite Jasmine. Made from a tree stump by a long-forgotten settler, it was finished with thick coats of clear varnish that had yellowed over the decades. Jasmine assumed it was varnish. There hadn't been any of it or paint on New Eden since before she was born. Hannah plunked down on it and patted the spot next to her. "Sit," she commanded Rodelle.

Rodelle rolled her eyes. "Do you really think both of us can fit on that thing?"

"We can each fit a butt cheek, so technically, yes."

"I deserve more than one butt cheek." Rodelle looked around the tack room, landing on a short stepladder hooked to the wall. She pulled it down and unfolded it next to Hannah. "There." She pushed the plate toward Jasmine. "Try them. Your guys brought back a ton of cooking supplies from the waystation, and I made these."

Jasmine folded the fabric and set it aside, then looked at the offerings on the dented metal plate. Her mouth watered. "Are these *doughnuts*?" Rolled dough hoops smeared with bright pink jam and sprinkled with sugar were artfully arranged on the plate. She'd never eaten them before, only read descriptions of the treats in old books.

"They are!" Rodelle beamed. "I managed to snag some sugar, flour, and cooking oil before the ship left again. There was a recipe in my great-grandmother's scrapbook, and with a couple of substitutions, I made these! I think they turned out pretty good, considering I didn't have any vanilla extract or maple syrup. They're sweet enough, anyway." She nodded at the plate. "Try one."

Jasmine picked up a pastry. "Where do you get maple syrup?"

"Old world trees. Maybe the cyborgs can figure out a way to synthesize it. I made the jam from sugar berries and a sweetener Brandon brought back from the waystation. What do you think?"

Jasmine took a cautious bite. A curious mix of sweetness and tartness exploded on her tongue. Despite their name, the sugar berries that were native to New Eden weren't particularly sweet. In the doughnuts, they had a rich taste, tempered by the dough, which had a crisp note to it. "Oh, my God," she moaned. "They're incredible."

"Aren't they great?" Hannah reached for one and ate half of it in one bite.

"What did you do to the bread dough?"

"It was lightly fried in oil," Rodelle replied. "Brandon helped with that part. He isn't sure how he knew, but he thinks one of his previous iterations may have enjoyed cooking." Her expression softened when she spoke about Brandon, piquing Jasmine's interest.

"What else does Brandon enjoy?" Jasmine asked, as casually as she could. Hannah bit back a smile.

Rodelle shrugged. "Cooking, talking. We've had a lot of chats around the backyard firepit."

"Is he still sleeping in your house?"

"Yeah, where else would he sleep?"

Jasmine caught Hannah's eye. "In your guesthouse with you?" Jasmine suggested.

"What? No, it's not like that." Rodelle seemed shocked at the suggestion. "We're friends, that's it. I'm too old for him, besides."

Once again, Jasmine and Hannah exchanged a look. "You're not too old," Hannah protested.

"You're only eight years older than me, and I don't think age is much of a concern for us at this point," Jasmine added.

"And that makes me too old for Brandon. I'm not looking to start a new relationship, anyway." Rodelle picked up a doughnut and took a delicate bite. The motion reminded Jasmine of being under Rodelle's care when she was little, of having little tea parties with wooden toys. Rodelle had chastised her and Hannah to sit up straight at the child-sized table and taught them which forks to use in what order, as if they would ever have a use for formal table manners.

The news that Rodelle preferred to remain single was a surprise to Jasmine. "Why not?"

Rodelle hesitated. Jasmine remembered her words days earlier, about how her marriage hadn't been what it appeared. She held her breath, waiting for Rodelle to reply. "There's a lot of freedom in being alone. I can see that now that I've managed to drag myself out of bed."

"Grief and depression do weird things to people," Hannah pointed out.

"They do, but it wasn't grief over Jackson's death that kept me a shut-in since the big quake. It was the planet's breakdown. It was our piss-poor excuse for the marriage itself." Rodelle's eyes became shiny. She looked away for a few seconds, blinking back tears. "We really didn't get along. My father was so desperate to see me paired off with a man. He didn't want me to be alone and knew how bad the New Eden population was getting. He and Jackson's parents thought we could help reestablish the population, get some babies in the mix, you know?" She shuddered. But whether it was the prospect of starting a family with so few resources available or having children at all, Jasmine couldn't tell.

"I couldn't get pregnant, anyway," Rodelle said miserably. "I don't know if it was him or me that had the problem, and I didn't care. It was a relief. Who the hell wants to raise children on fucking *New Eden*? They wouldn't even make it past infancy! I could've died in childbirth!" She brushed away tears before continuing. "Jackson had these delusions of grandeur that would have been a lot scarier if there were more people left. He talked about creating an empire, but there's nothing left here to create anything out of it. So, he turned our house into his own empire, and I was his only subject." Her words were bitter, tinged with pain.

Jasmine's breath caught. "What are you saying?"

"It was abusive. *Jackson* was abusive, emotionally and, occasionally, physically." Rodelle looked at her lap, where her hands were clenched together, her knuckles turning white.

She felt sick hearing the admission. "I had no idea . . ."

Rodelle barked out a short, humorless laugh. "That's a relief. I didn't want anyone to know, especially you two. I didn't want to put you in Jackson's line of fire."

"I'm so sorry," Hannah said softly. She had gone pale under her perpetual tan, eyes wide with shock.

"It's not your fault. There was a significant shortage of partners on this godforsaken rock, and when I was younger, I didn't want to go through the rest of my short, miserable existence alone if I didn't have to."

"It might not have been short," Hannah protested, but Rodelle cut her off.

"Our life expectancy isn't that great, between the natural disasters and lack of medicine. We have some hope now that the cyborg crew is here, although I'm sure we still have a long way to go toward having things like a proper hospital and doctors to staff it with." She wiped her eyes again, then tried to smile through her tears. "Anyway, now that I've told you how dangerous this place really is, I've decided to go on the expedition to the north."

Jasmine hadn't been expecting that. Neither had Hannah, judging by the surprised look on her face.

"I've never done anything fun in my life," Rodelle continued. "I've always done everything expected of me from my parents and Jackson, and it wasn't enough. I would like to experience one great adventure in my life before I die, and making a trek to the north will be it."

"You could've gone with the cyborgs to the waystation. It might've been safer than whatever's waiting in the north," Jasmine said.

Rodelle gave her a small smile through her tears. "Baby steps. I'm not ready to get on a spaceship yet. Checking out forbidden territory on a planet I'm already familiar with sounds better to me. And it isn't as if I'm going alone. I'll be with Brandon and CW44. We know there isn't any hostile wildlife in the north, so I don't have to worry about being bitten by something venomous." She sighed. "I just want to do something exciting for once."

"I get it. That's why I volunteered to go to the waysta-tion," Jasmine said.

"And why you have two boyfriends," Hannah added.

Jasmine felt a furious blush creep up her face. "Well, yeah. Highly recommended."

Hannah giggled. "How do you do it?"

"Well, none of us wanted to leave one out, and . . ."

"Don't tell me," Hannah said. "I changed my mind. I don't need the details. I'm happy the three of you worked something out." To Rodelle, she said, "Jasmine was pretty wrecked when she thought she would have to choose between Simon and Darius."

"I would be too, if I had to decide," Rodelle replied.

"You don't even want to be in a relationship," Jasmine said. She reached for another doughnut and took a bite. Heavenly.

"I don't, but if I did and I had two men who were at odds over me, I'd be into it."

Jasmine thought about how she awoke that morning, curled up between Simon and Darius on the makeshift bed of the couch and chaise. She chose her next words carefully, not wanting to speak too much about the relationship between Simon and Darius without them present. "I don't think they were at odds over me, exactly. There wasn't a lot of fighting or anything." They'd ended up fucking through their feelings instead.

"I'm glad it's working for you," Rodelle said. "I'm glad Hannah and Rhys have found each other too. As long as both of you remember that you don't have to do anything you don't want to. We don't owe the cyborgs our bodies in exchange for their help."

"I've never thought we did. I just wanted to climb Simon and Darius like trees when I met them, is all."

That earned a genuine laugh from Rodelle. "As long as you want to continue doing that, go for it. Just remember that you are your own person before being their partner. Same for you, Hannah." She changed the subject, gesturing to the folded piles of fabric. "I see you're already back in your element."

Jasmine smiled. "It's been so long since I had new cloth to work with. I've started making shirts. Everyone's been going around in rags for so long."

"Where did you find the patterns?" Hannah asked, touching a fragile piece of yellowed paper pinned to fabric. "I can't believe they're still intact!"

"I kept them under a floorboard. Less likely to get ripped up when they're out of the way. They made it through the quake."

"What's this?" Rodelle pulled out pink swaths of silky material from a box filled with fabric from the waystation.

"That was a present from Darius and Simon."

"It's beautiful!" Rodelle unfolded it and examined its

shimmer under the sunlight streaming through the tack room's window. "Do you have any more?"

"Just that piece. I was going to make a dress from it." She felt selfish at the admission, only making a single garment for herself from the nicest piece of fabric she had ever seen.

Rodelle raised a dark eyebrow. "Let me see the final product, at least. Assuming Simon and Darius don't tear it off you with their teeth."

Jasmine felt herself blush at the notion. She liked it very much. "Of course."

———

THE COMM UNIT'S speaker crackled, its first sign of life. Excitement welled in Simon as the static lowered while the unit searched for a deep space signal to latch onto. He had reset the unit so it would transmit on streams still in use by the rest of the galaxy. It beeped, the indicator light above the speaker glowing bright green. "It's online!" he said in excitement. He looked at Rhys, who stood next to him.

The ever-stoic cyborg nodded his head, the barest hint of a satisfied smile on his lips. "The unit will have to be replaced in the near future, but for now, it will suit our purposes. Hannah will be very pleased about this."

"What kind of range do you think it will ultimately get?" asked Simon.

"Perhaps the nearest waystation for now. Once it's been upgraded, there's no reason we wouldn't be able to communicate with anyone in the known universe."

An ominous shiver raced down Simon's spine. Of course, he knew of the universe outside this corner of the galaxy, but neither he nor the rest of his brethren ever desired to move into a more populated region. Their originals had been terrible people. There were probably still bounties on their heads somewhere. "Would we need to do that, though?"

Rhys gave an uncharacteristic half-shrug. "There are some friendly trading posts and stations relatively close by that would probably welcome a partnership with New Eden."

"What would New Eden offer? I doubt they'd be willing to give up their natural resources."

"A place to live. This is the only planet in this part of the galaxy habitable to humanoid life, or at least anyone who needs oxygen to breathe. The land is arable, and most of the water is fresh. There are people aboard stations who are sick of deep space living. It'll be safer after we've installed seismic activity monitors and constructed appropriate housing."

"What about the north?" Simon countered, thinking of the upcoming expedition. "It's nothing but caves."

"The caves are largely at the northernmost point of the landmass. There's a lot of space between it and the south. None of the current settlers have explored it. Which reminds me, we can use this to send a message to the crew aboard the ship." Rhys tapped the unit. "Ask them to run a full diagnostics on the northern part of the landmass before they break atmosphere."

"There could be something in the caves, maybe. Equipment they planned to use to make repairs later. A shuttle, who knows?" Possibilities raced through Simon's mind. He tried not to get his hopes too high, lest he decide to join the expedition. He needed to be with Darius and Jasmine as much as he needed air. "Medicine? Who knows what the first settlers hid out there that could have helped their families? Jasmine's parents?"

Rhys's next question was hesitant, as if he was nervous

about being told off. "Is everything all right between you—well, three, I suppose?"

Simon looked at him sharply.

Sheepishly, Rhys added, "Hannah and I don't keep secrets from each other. Hannah and Jasmine don't, either."

"Oh. Right." He made a mental note to ask Jasmine about Hannah the next time he saw her. "It's going well between us, I suppose. You don't want details, do you?"

"No, I'm being polite. I do care about you and want to see you happy."

"I don't know what we have," Simon admitted. "Just that it's very special to me. To all of us."

The comp screen that was awkwardly patched into the comm unit glowed for a moment as it came online. Rhys keyed in a couple of commands, running a diagnostic on the unit's addition. It was a newer comp from their ship and, thus far, seemed to be playing well with the outdated tech, albeit slower than any of them would have liked. "I'll send a message to the crew about the extended planetary analysis when the diagnostic is finished," he said. He looked around the room, as restored to its original condition as it was ever going to be.

Pride filled Simon when he thought of the tower, the work that had gone into it, and how it was going to transform New Eden lives for the better. Although after this, he was looking forward to returning to his agricultural duties, his first assignment when they arrived. He enjoyed getting his hands in the dirt and working under the twin suns.

"Is there anything else you need from me?" he asked.

Rhys gave him a knowing look, one dark eyebrow raised. "Eager to get back home?"

"Yes."

"Dismissed."

Simon paused in the doorway. The tower's spiral staircase had been swept clear of debris, its railing repaired. He turned around to face Rhys, whose gaze was still trained on the comm unit. "Rhys?"

"Yes?"

"Do you think we should all have dinner together soon?"

"Why?"

Simon sighed. Of all of them, Rhys was the most robotic, the most detached from his humanity, at least when he was away from Hannah. "Because it's what friends who are couples do sometimes."

"Even if one couple has an extra person?"

"No, that implies that one of us doesn't belong." Simon couldn't imagine not being with Jasmine and Darius. What had once been an unattainable dream was now his reality, his reasons for living. "Damn it, Rhys, I'm trying to be nice."

"Oh! I see. Then, yes, I suppose we should share dinner together sometime soon. Perhaps after we've stabilized the rest of the buildings against seismic activity."

This was as good an answer as Simon was likely to get from Rhys. "Thank you."

CHAPTER THIRTEEN

Two DAYS PASSED before the ship returned, shuddering into place on a freshly rebuilt launchpad near the comms tower. It arrived after breakfast, an event that had most of the settlement collected at the landing site, eager to see what had been brought back in its cargo holds.

And eager to help, Jasmine thought as she surveyed the crowd. This supply run was bigger than the one she'd accompanied, the crew having gone to more far-flung destinations. The New Edeners fully realized the scope of the trip when the starboard hold opened and giant anti-grav cages glided out, holding baby cows and draft horses.

Jasmine couldn't stop herself. She squealed in delight and raced for the cages, Hannah at her heels. A black and white calf mooed at her plaintively from her bed of straw. "I hope we're not going to eat you," she said by way of greeting.

"No one's eating the cows yet," Hannah said from behind her. "They're cloned animals, meant to get our agricultural production up and running. They'll provide milk when they're older."

Jasmine peered at the animals' cages. "I haven't seen a cow like this, ever. The ones who died in the quake didn't look like this."

"That's because those were cross-breeds from other similar species from the old world's solar system. I think these might actually be purebred clones from the old world," Hannah said in awe. She bent down to better see the calf. "Oh, my God. She's adorable!"

A cyborg, who'd named himself Daniel, strode down the cargo bay's ramp, guiding anti-grav pallets loaded with tools and boxes. "They're old world purebred clones. Guernseys," he confirmed, meeting Hannah's gaze. "Sorry, couldn't help but overhear."

"And they're healthy?" Hannah shuffled to another cage to look at one of the horses.

"Very much so."

"I'm appreciative of the animals, but is there any machinery onboard?" Hannah asked.

Jasmine shot her a look that questioned her intelligence. "Who cares about that? When was the last time we had actual animals other than chickens?" She wagged her fingers at the black and white calf, who *lowed* in response. "I'm going to call you Daisy."

"We have some with us, but there's the practical aspect to consider," Daniel replied. "We don't have the infrastructure in place yet to handle large-scale automated production, nor do we have the population. I'm sure we'll get there eventually, but it didn't make sense to spend a lot of credits on things that are going to be shut away until it's feasible to use them."

"Good point." Hannah sighed. "I was thinking about how we're going to care for the animals. And by 'we,' I mean me."

"Nothing to worry about on that front. There's a lot

more help available with food production now that the comms tower is back online and we've returned. Besides, they came with instructions."

"The cows we used to have only needed to be fed every thirty-six hours," Hannah said doubtfully.

"These will need to be fed more than that. It's all right —we brought back plenty of feed. We also have cloned cells for chickens. They can go into a tank at any time. Fish cells, too."

Jasmine's excitement rose again. "Fish? What kind?"

"But the ecosystem . . ." Hannah protested.

"The ecosystem won't be disturbed if the fish are contained in their own ponds and tanks," Daniel replied. To Jasmine, he said, "They're gritzels. Hardy freshwater fish native to Inkhil-Four. Of course, we can't release them into the oceans and waterways, at least not until we've had a chance to do a proper survey of them, but we can certainly set up a pool or pond."

A grinding noise sounded as the ship's exterior door opened and its ramp extended. More anti-grav pallets and flitters emerged, loaded with stuff, and Jasmine quickly got out of the way. Hannah leapt into action, giving directions and issuing instructions. Feeling useless, Jasmine stood back, looking in the direction of the launchpad that was still under construction. The rest of the materials needed to repair it had to be aboard the ship.

"She's really taken over, even though she says she doesn't want to."

Ollie's voice was unmistakable. Jasmine rolled her eyes before turning around. "Someone had to take some initiative," she snapped. "Hannah's the whole reason the cyborgs are here in the first place." She fought to keep her temper in check, not wanting to start an argument yet. Being neighbors, there was plenty of time for that.

"She did. I hope things get easier for her now that we have supplies."

Shocked into silence, Jasmine gawked at him. When she found her voice, all she could say was, "What?"

"Easier for her," Ollie repeated, like she was simple.

"When have you cared about life being easier for her? You used to wake her up in the morning to complain."

"That was to keep her on her toes."

"That's a fucked-up thing to do. You could've helped more, you know." She refrained from saying anything else, not wanting to be the target of his harassment. "There's an expedition going to the north. Maybe you could volunteer to go," she added.

"I'm too old to be stomping around in the dirt."

"You can still help, and failing that, just keep your opinions to yourself," Jasmine shot back. Her good mood at seeing the animals evaporated. She looked around the crowd for Simon or Darius, but didn't see either. They were probably in the comms tower, double checking that everything was working.

Ollie was quiet for a few seconds, and she wondered if he was hurt. Finally, he said, "We're all bad at this, aren't we?"

"What do you mean?"

"Surviving. All of us, we're terrible at it. At least you and Hannah have each other. I keep staying alive when, by all odds, I should've died after a tree branch fell on me long ago. Beats the hell out of me why I'm still here."

"So, you're determined to be rude and difficult as revenge for not dying?"

"I suppose I've been doing that." Ollie sounded uncharacteristically remorseful. "Do you know what it's like to outlive everyone and be surrounded by children on a dying planet?"

It was on the tip of Jasmine's tongue to tell Ollie that the planet itself was thriving, if not winning a war against its human inhabitants, thanks to its earthquakes. But she didn't, her curiosity having been piqued. Sympathy, as well, which she didn't expect. "I guess not."

"I'm old enough to be your grandfather. I'm the last of my kind. It's awful."

"You've fussed about every bit of progress the cyborgs have brought with them."

"I have, and I probably shouldn't." He sighed. "I suppose I'm tired of being alive. Promise me you won't save me if I fall down."

"What? No, I won't promise that. You drive me nuts, but I wouldn't let you die."

"I'm bored and I've lived too long."

"If you're bored, you probably shouldn't have suggested burning all books for cooking fires back in the day." She couldn't help herself from getting that dig in as the memory of his stomping through the settlement returned. The memory still made her angry. He'd been on a tear, not wanting to cut down a tree for firewood, one of the few things New Eden had in relative abundance.

He shrugged. "You're right about that." He actually sounded contrite for the first time.

Now it was Jasmine's turn to sigh. She hoped she wouldn't regret what she was about to say. "I brought back a lot of them from my trip to the waystation. I was going to set them up in a library once we've figured out where a good spot would be. Do you want to borrow a couple sometime?"

Ollie tilted his head in surprise. "You'd let me read them? I promise I won't burn them."

"I'll kill you myself if you do."

He actually chuckled, and Jasmine stared at him in

shock. "I don't doubt it. Either you or your . . . friends." He squinted at her. "Are they your friends? They seem to have moved in with you."

"Simon was already living with me before my house all but fell over."

"Whatever works for you three."

She hadn't been expecting that response. She stared at him, agog. "You were completely against our hosting the cyborgs."

"I was wrong to do so."

"You should probably tell Hannah that."

"I will, once she's finished wrangling that horse." He nodded at Hannah, who held a hand out to one of the baby horses, now released from its cage. The animal nuzzled her fingers, drawing a smile of delight from her. "Just because I don't expect to live much longer doesn't mean the rest of you shouldn't get a shot at surviving as long as I have."

Once again, Jasmine didn't have a response to that. Before she could ask Ollie what the hell had happened to him to change so much, he shuffled away, cooing at one of the calves in a high-pitched warble she'd never heard from him before.

Weird. She turned back to the ship, looking for something she could help with, but everything seemed to be under control. Loaded anti-grav pallets zipped in all directions, delivering precious supplies around the settlement. With nothing else to do, she headed for the comms tower, eager to see what it looked like inside.

Its original heavy wooden door was still in place, and it slammed shut behind with an air of finality that made her shudder. The air was cooler in the tower's foyer. It took a few seconds for her vision to adjust to the dim light offered by the lights powered by cyborgs' weird perpetual batteries.

The spiral stairs leading to the control room had been repaired and the floors cleaned. Grasping the railing, she climbed up, pausing halfway up after getting dizzy.

A murmur of voices greeted her when she stepped on the landing. To her left and right were supply closets, the doors long gone. Peeking inside, she saw they were empty of the refuse that had been piled inside them for decades. Beside the closet on her right was a small room with a rusted-out cot inside, stripped of a mattress or bedding. Immediately ahead of her was a narrow hallway, with the control room itself at the end. She strode down it, finding Rhys and Simon inside. The room's giant window that overlooked the launchpad was freshly cleaned, the hulking ship visible through its deep blue tint. The control panels shone and tiny lights dotting it blinked at irregular intervals, making Jasmine never want to touch them for fear of breaking something. "Wow," she said in appreciation.

Rhys and Simon finally noticed her. Their expressions were stricken, almost panicked. Fear flared in her. "What happened?"

"Nothing yet." Simon quickly crossed the room to embrace her, heedless of Rhys. "We just received a transmission, is all."

Her panic quickly gave way to relief. "Isn't that the point of having a comms tower?"

"It is, but this is unusual. It was a timed transmission, meant to be opened by the New Eden authorities over a hundred years ago. It's only now unpacked since the tower was brought back online."

"So, does this mean the original settlers were definitely criminals?"

"It could be." Simon's expression was unreadable. He stumbled over his next words, exchanging an unreadable look with Rhys. "Well, it's in code, but we were able to break it. The original settlers owed other people financially, and it appears the settlers reneged on the deal." He took a deep breath. "There's an obsolete origin code attached to it. It's from our ship."

———

SIMON HELD HIS BREATH. Dimly, he was aware of his cybernetics reminding him of the need to inhale, an ever-present reminder that he wasn't fully human.

Jasmine's eyes were huge, and he knew if he conducted a diagnostic on her, she would be just as breathless as he was. As it was, he didn't want to touch her, for fear of . . . what? That she would push him away? None of what had happened with and to New Eden was her fault, or his. His previous self, maybe, but . . .

Pain lanced his enhanced heart. Simon had more in common with his shitbag original than Jasmine did with her forebears. He waited for her to speak, to say anything that might assuage his terror in that moment. He wouldn't be able to bear it if she hated him and Darius.

"Jasmine?" he said, a cautious note in his voice.

"Yeah?" She shook her head, as if to clear her thoughts.

"Are you upset?"

"Why the hell would I be upset? Your clones did business with the first settlers, and they got ripped off. I'm not even as surprised as I feel like I should be."

Simon stared at her, aghast.

"*You* didn't personally come to collect," Jasmine continued nonchalantly. "What does the message say, exactly? Read it out loud."

Simon turned back to the message. "'Payment is expected to be made in seventy-two hours.' The landing coordinates match what would have been the old launch-pad, and the origin code is definitely from our ship."

"Maybe your clones didn't write it at all," Jasmine suggested. "You said it arrived a hundred years ago."

"Our previous clones were in possession of that ship a century ago. It's been modified since then, but . . ."

"But what? Our great-great grandparents ripped off your previous clones. Obviously your clones didn't do anything to New Eden, because we're standing here right now, and then everyone went on to live their lives." She looked at the comms equipment with more disinterest than he would have had if their positions had been reversed. "You had nothing to do with this. None of us did. We've been over this, multiple times. Your originals rebelled against whatever fucked-up program they signed up for. They did the right thing in the end."

"But the first clones may not have," Simon protested.

"Oh, my God, why are you arguing with me? Haven't we all hashed this out about a dozen times by now? Rhys nearly keeled over, remember?" Jasmine gave a frustrated sigh. She put her hands on either side of his face, as if she thought he might run away. "I'm not going to abandon you because your previous clones might have done business with my great-great-grandparents or whoever. I hope you and Darius aren't going to take off because my people may have double-crossed yours." She glanced at Rhys, as if suddenly remembering he was standing there. "I take it Hannah has told you about the three of us?"

Rhys looked at Simon, as if searching for permission, probably remembering their late night chat so long ago, when Simon told him about his feelings for Jasmine and Darius. "Yes."

Was it Simon's imagination, or was Rhys *blushing*? He felt some of the tension in his shoulders relax. Jasmine hadn't moved her hands, and he put his over them, needing the connection. "Thank you," he murmured.

"What for?"

"Just—for being you. For not being upset about this. It means a lot to me."

"Rhys, could you give us a minute?" Jasmine asked.

Rhys blinked owlishly, genuine confusion crossing his face. Of the entire crew, he had always been the stiffest, the least receptive to human emotions and social cues. "A minute," he said. "Of course." After a brief nod, he left the room.

"You know he'll be gone for exactly one minute," Simon said.

"Yeah, so we'd better make this quick." She let go of him to put her hands on her hips. "You're being dramatic again."

He hadn't expected that. "I'm sorry?"

"Maybe 'dramatic' is a little insensitive. You're in the weeds again. It feels like you're looking for an excuse for me to leave you."

He was horrified at the notion. "I'm not!"

"You are. You keep putting out reasons for why we shouldn't be together, trying to make yourself sound as unappealing as possible. You're worried about what others will think, you're worried about Darius, you're worried about me being angry over something that happened who-knows-how-many-years before I was born and possibly before you were hatched."

"We aren't exactly hatched."

"Swam out of your tank, I don't know." She sighed and her voice softened. "You keep stressing yourself out about the what-ifs. And that's important, as long as it doesn't get in the way of living. You guys came here for a better life. You should enjoy it sometimes."

"I do." He reached for her hands and brought them to his lips. Emotion clogged his throat. "My time here has been the happiest I've ever had in my life, more so with you and Darius. I never imagined I'd have both of you at my side."

"Either side. We're on either side of you. Or both of you are on either side of me. I like being the filling in a Simon-Darius sandwich."

The control room door opened and Rhys stepped in. "It's been over a minute."

"Oh, my God," muttered Jasmine.

"Were either of you planning on a dinner invitation tonight? I thought I heard you speak of sandwiches."

"You wouldn't be interested in the kind we're talking about," said Jasmine.

"Get out, Rhys," ordered Simon.

Rhys gave them a puzzled look, but stepped away, closing the door behind him.

Jasmine looked like she was trying to keep herself from laughing. She leaned into him. "Relax a little," she said. "I know you're distressed about what might've happened here a hundred years ago, but I'm not. I'm curious. Now I really want to go on that expedition."

Simon leaned his forehead against hers, then curled his hands around her fingers, so delicate and fragile. "Absolutely not. It'll be too dangerous. I have no idea what the terrain is like, and I couldn't live with myself if anything happened to you or Darius."

"The next one, then."

He would argue about that with her if another expedition came up. "The next one."

CHAPTER FOURTEEN

THE THREE OF them had a cookout in the front yard for supper, siting on the ground together, as they waited for their food. The fire gave off a pleasant heat, its flames licking over the vegetable chunks Jasmine had speared over a sharpened stick. When the pepper slices and carrot pieces were sufficiently blackened, she sprinkled a few pinches of powdered seasoning on them, one of the things brought back from the last trip off-world. Whenever she thought about the stuff the crew brought back this time, a wave of selfishness crested over her. She'd been so focused on exploring the spaceship and waystation, and later Darius and Simon's bodies, as well as acquiring fabric and books for herself. The other crew who made the journey brought back more practical things everyone could share.

She did note with satisfaction and relief that a few New Edeners were already wearing the new tunics she'd made in the barn's tack room over the last couple of days. The garments were easy enough to put together. She felt a little less useless seeing Rodelle wearing one, belted at the waist with a cord made from braided fabric scraps, the hem of her shorts dangling underneath, when she took off on the northern expedition. Even Ollie had been pleased to receive one when Jasmine brought it over that afternoon. She figured it was a type of insurance, a way to keep him from bothering her for a while.

Simon wore one in lieu of his black cyborg uniform shirt. Bits of metal embedded in his skin flashed, glinting in the setting suns' light. He tossed some kindling on the fire, stoking the flames a little higher. "I think it's good," Darius said from his spot on the scrubby grass next to Jasmine.

Simon glared at it critically. "Could be bigger."

"It's fine," Jasmine said. "Come eat with us."

The remark drew a raised eyebrow from Simon. "Move over," he said, squeezing himself between her and Darius. He accepted a proffered stick, loaded with carrot pieces and salt. "No tomatoes?" He pretended to pout as he held it over the fire.

"Darius polished off the tomato stash." Jasmine worked one off her stick and held it in front of Simon's lips. He ate it with a nod, the brief feel of his mouth around her fingers drawing a shiver from her, despite the lingering warmth of the day.

"Not quite. There are a few hundred left in the barn. I grew them, I would know." Simon kept his eyes trained on the fire.

"Will you be going back to agricultural production now that the comms tower is finished?" Jasmine asked.

He shrugged. "I'd like to, but I'll go wherever I'm needed."

"The sickbay is up and running, sort of, so that's most of the major infrastructure," Darius said.

"Clinic," Jasmine corrected him.

"Sickbay, clinic, same thing. New Eden definitely needs a real hospital and a qualified doctor or two, though. I think I heard Rhys and Hannah talking about putting out a call or SOS or something for medical personnel elsewhere in the galaxy."

A thrill coursed through Jasmine at the possibility. "More people!"

Darius poked her in the side, in a ticklish spot. She nearly dropped her stick. "We aren't enough for you?"

"You are, and you know it. New Eden needs more *people*, if we're going to survive another generation or two. Genetic diversity and all." She fished a piece of carrot off the stick and popped it into her mouth. "Do you want to talk about what we found out at the comms tower today? Simon was pretty put out about it."

"You know more about biology than I'd expect for someone who grew up on an isolated planet without electricity," Simon commented.

"We had electricity until the major quake two years ago. A library with books from the old world too. Things had been going downhill for years before, but it didn't really ramp up until the quake. And you didn't answer my question."

Darius reached for her free hand and squeezed it. "We have no way of knowing anything else about that coincidence yet." That revelation had been kept between them, Rhys, and Hannah. There was nothing else in the century-old transmission that explained the New Eden and cyborg connection or apparent business deal that had gone wrong. The coded message hadn't been threatening, just a query about payment for something that had been sent before the comms tower was deactivated. Telling everyone else about the discovery before they knew all the facts would only cause more upset.

"Maybe it is just a coincidence. Hell of one, though," Jasmine replied.

"Or not, if our iterations during that time were likely nomadic. It would make sense that they would conduct business with other isolated people," Simon said. Now that he knew their previous clones hadn't been cruel to New Eden, he sounded much more relaxed about that bit of news,.

"That makes sense, I guess." She looked behind her at the house, a sudden stab of grief piercing her heart at the sight. The message forgotten, she thought about her old home, condemned and in pieces. The last thing she'd had of her family.

Something in her expression must have given her away, because Darius said quietly, "You miss them and the house, don't you?"

Unexpected and unwelcome tears filled her eyes. "Yeah. I wish my parents could have met you." Before either of them could ask if they would have approved of their relationship, she quickly added, "They wanted me to be happy, no matter what. I'm sure they would have liked both of you."

"What were they like?" Simon asked.

A picture of her parents came to mind, before her mother was sick. Both of them tall, her father perpetually sunburned, his white-blond hair a match for Jasmine's. Her mother, slender, auburn-haired, dark-eyed. Both of them were as happy as they could be in their marriage arranged by the New Eden council, the couple pushed together due to their close age and lack of genetic relations. "Pleasant" was the word Jasmine used to describe them. "They accepted their lot in life."

Both of them looked at her quizzically.

It took a few seconds for Jasmine to collect herself and remember the murky details her parents had given her about their marriage. "They were friends growing up, I think. Grew up down the street from each other."

"This one?" Simon asked.

She shook her head. "An older one closer to the power station that was torn down before I was born. If you dig in the right spot, you'll find foundations still buried. I think, at some point, the council got worried about flooding. Anyway, Dad and Mum were childhood friends. Since they were the right ages and got along well enough, the council decided they should be married."

"Was that how it always worked?" Darius asked.

"I'm not sure. I think in the earliest days of the settlement, people could choose if and when they married. That changed as the population died off."

"One of the many ways your predecessors fucked up," Darius remarked. "Speaking of genetic diversity."

"No one's been inbred. The original settlers set up a program to make sure that didn't happen," Jasmine insisted. "I don't have a grand sister in my family tree."

That remark drew smiles from both of them.

"I'm glad you're here," she said, a serious note to her voice. "Not just because of *this*." She waved her hands around the three of them. "You've brought hope to New Eden for the first time in my lifetime. You know how kids think they're immortal?"

"I haven't spent any time around children," Darius said.

"Neither have I," Simon added.

"What about when you were kids?" Jasmine asked.

"Neither of us were. We woke up in the cloning tank as adults, had our hardware activated, then two months, was it? Maybe three?" Darius looked at Simon for confirmation, who nodded. "Two or three months of rigorous mental and physical training."

Jasmine forgot about New Eden's plight for a few seconds, fascinated with this tidbit of information. "You were born fully grown but had training?"

"To be people, basically," Darius explained. "I sort of remember waking up in the tank, knowing that I exist and how to breathe and then being kind of terrified by it." His expression darkened. "It was horrifying. If there had been a way to preserve previous clones' memories or traits or something, or a program to ease the way into existing, maybe it would have been easier." He patted Simon's knee. "This guy was right here when I came to—I remember that."

"Is that why you two were together?" Jasmine couldn't help but ask.

They exchanged a look before turning back to her. "We weren't, except for that one-night stand, until we met you," Simon replied. "I think our originals or previous clones might have been couples, but we don't know for sure."

"And there's nothing on your ship about them," Jasmine said. They shook their heads. "Fucking incredible, in a bad way. At least I can remember where I came from." She hated to remind them that they didn't know their origins for certain, only that whatever their originals had been, it couldn't have been good.

Simon gave a half-shrug. "We're together. That's what I care about the most." He brought the subject back around to Jasmine. "Your parents wouldn't have minded us?"

"I doubt it. Our situation is a bit unusual, but I think they would have welcomed change. My mother—she started to go a little stir-crazy before she died." A lump formed in her throat. She had to talk around it. "It was the boredom more than anything. Nothing but endless sun, heat, and tremors beneath your feet that you couldn't do anything about. No entertainment, except plays in the amphitheater or re-reading the same books."

Her mother would fall to tears at random, clutching Jasmine or her father like they were her lifelines. She'd never uttered the wish that she wanted to leave; it had seemed impossible. Her mother had just given up shortly before she died. She'd even smiled a few times on her deathbed, muttering about how she would soon be free. The memory still hurt Jasmine's heart.

"I understood the boredom a lot better when I became an adult. I think all of us were just milling around waiting to die, except Hannah. We *would* have died, if not for her. So would you, eventually, after your asteroid was destroyed." Not wanting to fall to pieces just yet, she changed the subject. "What was the asteroid like?"

"Dull and colorless," Darius replied. "Talking to each other in our heads, sometimes making a supply run to one of the waystations logged in our navigation systems. AS36 has a couple decks of cards, so sometimes, we'd play rounds of Stars and Kings."

"We didn't venture too far from the stations that were friendly to us," Simon added. "We're pretty sure our originals and first clones burned a lot of bridges with other planets and stations, and we didn't want to draw attention to ourselves."

Jasmine had heard about that before. "We're alike in a lot of ways. None of us really know where we come from, now that we know the original settlers probably didn't come here to escape the dangers of modern society." She didn't intend for her words to come out as bitterly as they did.

Darius and Simon only nodded. At least they could understand why she was so upset, how that revelation had shaken New Eden's straggling population to its core.

"I feel like all this suffering of the later generations was for nothing," she added.

Darius wrapped an arm around her and squeezed. Simon scooted to her other side to do the same. She leaned into them, needing the contact, the reassurance that she wasn't wrong to feel this way. Neither of them tried to comfort her with worthless platitudes about how at least they were together now. She was allowed to be angry about what had happened to her people, thanks to the selfishness and short-sightedness of their predecessors. She was allowed to grieve the deaths of her parents, who might have lived had proper medical care been possible.

They stayed that way for what felt like hours. Silent tears ran down Jasmine's face, blurring her view of the fire. She let herself grieve for what she and New Eden had lost and could never reclaim.

IT WAS dusk by the time they packed up their things to go back to the house. Jasmine was quiet, flanked on either side by Simon and Darius. Simon felt as if a pall had been cast over them, a specter of their respective pasts that would always be there. He didn't have the desire to know what kind of person his original had been or where he had come from. His original had willingly enrolled in a shadowy military program for money. He'd been motivated by greed. Simon had no desire to learn more about a man who could do such a thing.

But all Jasmine's poor parents had done was to be born in the wrong place at the wrong time.

I want all of us to go to bed.

Darius's voice in his head nearly had Simon stumbling over the house's threshold. He'd been dropped out of their shared link for so long that he'd almost managed to forget it existed. "*Sex isn't exactly on my mind right now,*" he replied, a little peevishly.

Darius's response was affronted. "*It isn't on mine, either. We're all feeling a little down. Let's get in bed and cuddle together, yeah?*"

Jasmine switched on the battery-powered lamps. "I really don't like it when you two speak telepathically without me," she said. "I can tell, you know. Your eyes kind of go blank."

"Darius started it."

That drew a small smile from her. "Thank you for listening," she said softly. "I didn't mean to fall apart like that."

"If you can't fall apart around your boyfriends, when can you?" Darius asked.

She brightened a little, some of the sparkle returning to her eyes. "You know, I never in a million years thought I'd get to have *one* boyfriend, let alone two. I'm really glad I didn't have to choose between you two."

Simon's heart lurched at the thought of it, as it always did when he pondered not having one of them with him.

"What were you two talking about in your heads, anyway?" she asked suspiciously.

"About how I'd like to lie in bed together and breathe, mostly," Darius replied.

"Really? Just that?"

"You know, we like you for you, not just what you do for us in bed," Simon said. Lies. He loved them both. But he'd never told anyone he loved them and wasn't sure how to now. How the hell did one bring that up in conversation organically?

My parents died because of a lack of medical care caused by thoughtless smugglers who left their descendants stranded.

That's terrible. I love you, Jasmine. I love you, Darius.

Decidedly inappropriate.

Jasmine's shoulders sank in relief for a few seconds. "I think I have a bottle of dandelion wine around here," she said. "Want some?"

"Sure," Darius automatically replied. Simon nodded.

"I guess you have antidote programs that'll flush it out, not that the alcohol content is that high." Jasmine rooted around the kitchen cabinets for cups and a bottle of the homemade wine that was so prevalent on New Eden. Simon had had it before. She was right; the alcohol content was low. That had to be a good thing on a planet where boredom reigned.

"We can switch them off," Simon replied.

"No one's getting bombed on it, anyway." Jasmine poured three cups' worth of dandelion wine and handed two to them. "I like your idea of lying in bed, nursing our collective misery. Let's go." Her tone was lighter, despite the weight of her words. Simon wondered how long it had been since she'd been able to vent, if ever.

They followed her to the living room, where their makeshift bed was still set up, the covers mussed. Setting down her cup on a side table, Jasmine stripped off her clothes and crawled in. The sight of her bare skin would always make Simon's heartbeat notch up a little, and when he glanced at Darius, the expression on his face told him he thought the same. She was the most beautiful thing either of them had ever seen.

They did likewise, shucking their clothing. They settled in the improvised bed on either side of her, Darius drawing the thin sheet over their bodies. Simon pressed a kiss to her temple. "What else did you want to talk about?" he asked. "We're all ears."

"That was it," she replied. "I'm angry about what

happened to New Eden but happy I met you two. The entire cyborg crew, actually. You've brought us back to life."

"Ironic, considering we're from a lifeless terraformed asteroid," Darius quipped.

"You never did tell me more about what it was like."

"Much like our ship. Lots of sleeping pods, few comforts. Very utilitarian," Simon said.

"Yeah, I was wondering about that. Why didn't any of you use the real beds aboard your ship?"

"It's more efficient to be in the pods. Closer to the bridge and the cargo bays. We know previous clones acquired the ship from someone else, and they probably didn't want to avail themselves of creature comforts, you know? Probably some fucked-up form of cybernetic superiority over organic humans." Simon snuggled deeper in the blankets and put his hand on her belly, concentrating on the way it rose and fell in breath. She gave a little sigh of pleasure.

"They felt like bad luck to me," Darius added. "Like, if we used them, we'd have to acknowledge that someone before us did some terrible things to get the ship. The databanks were erased of identifying details."

"And you don't know who did the erasing?" Jasmine asked.

"No."

"Maybe it wasn't you. Are you the most advanced people in the universe? There has to be someone out there who has that knowledge," she suggested. She sounded wistful, like she didn't want to believe that cyborgs could be capable of wreaking devastation across the universe. They weren't now, of course, but they couldn't say the same for the previous clones or originals.

"It's very possible, I suppose. Although I doubt we're

the most advanced species in the universe. I feel like that's kind of subjective," Simon replied.

Jasmine sat up a little. The thin sheet slipped down, revealing her breasts, which caught Simon's attention. His body stirred. When he managed to tear his gaze away for half a second, he noticed Darius's zooming in on her too. "How is advancement subjective? You can fly through space. You probably have access to all the medicine in the known universe, and if you don't, you know where to get it or make it. You invented those weird batteries that never run out. I'm not complaining about them, mind you. They're fucking incredible! You clone yourselves!" A pause, then she cleared her throat. "Gentlemen, my eyes are up here."

Both of them looked up to meet her amused expression.

Simon had to remind himself what they were talking about in the first place. "Advancement isn't just about space travel and cybernetic organs. There's a level of, well, *humanity*, I guess, to consider too. Diplomacy."

"And there's such a civilization out there that has achieved tech advances and, I don't know, peacekeeping together?"

"Probably, although I couldn't name one," Simon replied. He didn't want to talk about advancements in technology anymore, not when he was naked in bed—sort of—with the two people he loved more than anything else in the universe. His whole body ached with need for them.

And yet, they'd started off in bed as a means of comfort while commiserating over past grief. Guilt twinged through him, warring with lust.

Jasmine heaved a dramatic sigh. "Maybe we should've stayed outside."

"I'm very happy here." Darius snuggled into her, laying

his head over her chest. Jasmine's hand stroked through his hair.

"I don't feel like crying anymore, and I don't think either of you do, either." She gave a pointed look at them in turn. Simon couldn't keep himself from smiling. He knew she wasn't really upset. "Anyway, through my blubbering outside, I forgot to tell you I made something just for us. Well, me. But you get to see it." Before either of them could reply, she hauled herself up and crawled over the furniture. Simon leaned back to enjoy the view of her ass as she scampered barefoot up the stairs.

"Stunning," said Darius appreciatively.

Simon had to agree.

A couple of minutes later, she descended the stairs, wearing a . . . well, technically it was a dress. Two wide straps crisscrossed over her breasts, wrapping around her hips to gather in a skirt that fell a few centimeters above her knees. When she slowly turned around in a circle, they could see the straps were tied in a knot around the back of her neck, like she was a present to be unwrapped. "What do you think?" she asked. Her eyes sparkled. "I made it this afternoon. I was going to surprise you with this tonight, before we got naked, but I guess we got ahead of ourselves."

Simon's mouth went dry. It took a few seconds for him to find his voice. "Promise me you will never wear that outside this house." His tone came out sharper than he intended.

Hurt flashed across her features.

"That's only for us," Darius said gently.

She brightened again. "Do you remember when we bought this?"

Simon vaguely remembered buying the pink fabric back at the waystation's concourse, but the need to be inside her as soon as possible obliterated any memories of that moment. He tried to convey that in the look he sent her.

She gave them a devilish look. She knew exactly what she was doing.

Jasmine crawled back on the bed. She sat up on her haunches between them and traced a finger along their chests, drawing shuddering breaths from each. Simon had to fight his instincts to rip away her dress's straps but bunched his hands in the sheets, waiting for her to take this further. He didn't have to look at Darius or speak to him over their shared link to know he was feeling the same, or that his pulse had to be picking up speed.

"I don't know who to kiss first," she said.

"It doesn't matter. You won't hurt our feelings, as long as we both get a turn," Darius said.

Jasmine covered her eyes with one hand. With the other, she pointed at each in turn, muttering a rhyme Simon didn't recognize. She stopped with her finger pointed at him and raised her other hand. Simon's breath caught, his internal comp alerting him to the changes in his body. He ignored it and pulled her to him.

Her kiss was electric, the feel of her dress's silky material against his skin almost frustrating. The bed dipped as Darius moved toward them, hand sliding around Jasmine as he levered himself up on his side to get closer to them. Jasmine's breath mingled with theirs as she shifted her face to Darius's, pressing a kiss to his lips. She broke the contact with both and sat up again, skin flushed. Pushing her hair over her shoulder to grab the dress's straps at the back of her neck, she unknotted them to reveal her breasts. Even though he'd seen them before, Simon would never tire of the sight. Without thinking, he reached for his cock, already hard with wanting for both of them.

"I want you both inside me," she said quickly. "I thought about it, and I'd like to try it." Her words came out in a rush, like she thought they might decline such a suggestion.

Simon and Darius exchanged a quick glance. Darius's eyes were wide, glazed over at the very idea, and Simon knew he had to look the same. "I think all of us would like that," he said, voice strangled. He moved his hand to her breast, kneading the soft flesh and plucking at her nipple. Mirroring his movement, Darius did the same with the other one. "We'll be gentle," Simon promised.

As if on cue, Darius rose and got out of the bed. "I'll be right back," he promised. "Don't get started without me." Metalwork in his back shone under the battery-powered lamplight, contrasted with his well-honed muscles.

"Like I'd do that," Jasmine muttered. She pulled down the sheet to reveal Simon's bare body. Licking her lips, she reached for his cock and stroked it from base to tip, drawing a harsh breath from him.

"I think that counts," he gasped.

"Do you want me to stop?"

"God, no. Just . . . don't go any further until Darius gets back."

According to his internal comp, it was only a few seconds, but it felt like hours before Darius returned, a small bottle in hand. Simon recognized it from their night together at the waystation before they arrived on New Eden. "What's that?" Jasmine asked curiously.

"Oil."

Understanding dawned on her face. She blushed, which Simon didn't know was possible at this point. "Oh."

"He'll make it good for you," Simon promised.

"Like he did for you?"

"Yes," he and Darius replied simultaneously. Simon fought back a chuckle. Darius grinned.

She nodded, a knowing, almost shy smile on her face as she straddled Simon's hips, skirt fabric bunched in her hand. She hovered over him before grasping his shaft, angling her body over his. Her eyes were heavy-lidded with lust, yet her expression was nearly thoughtful as she lowered herself on to him. His breath came out in a hiss as she slowly sank down, embracing him in her wet heat. "Ohhh," she groaned.

Pressing her hands on his chest, she experimentally slid up and dropped back down on him, a motion that he couldn't help but mimic. His hips thrust upward, drawing another moan from her, the noise making him fight for control sooner than he'd expected. He gripped her hips through the pink fabric, the uncivilized part of him wishing to rip away the material; another part of him found the sight of her half-undressed and disheveled unbearably sexy.

From behind her, Darius brushed her hair aside to kiss her neck, teeth lightly scraping her skin. His hands had disappeared under her skirt, and Simon knew he had to be coating his fingers with oil to prepare her. He remembered when Darius had done the same for him, and he froze for half a second, the memory alone nearly enough to bring him to orgasm.

If Jasmine noticed his body stilling, she didn't let on. She had paused in riding him.

Darius's face was fixed in concentration as he entered her with his fingers. "How is it?" he murmured.

"I think I like it," she said hoarsely. "It's different, but I like it."

"Tell me if you want me to stop."

"I will." She laughed, a breathless noise. "I don't think

I'll be doing that, though."

His body under control for now, Simon thrust into her. Jasmine's eyes nearly rolled into the back of her head. "He's very good at that," Simon said through gritted teeth.

"He did this for you?" Jasmine's hips rolled against him as Darius thrust his fingers into her.

"He did."

"I'd like to see that sometime."

"That can be arranged," Darius said.

A shudder of pleasure rippled through Simon at the idea.

Jasmine paused, her breath catching again. "Relax," Darius whispered.

She nodded, moving forward to give him better access. Now it was Simon's turn to forget to breathe as Darius squeezed more oil on his hands, the sound wet. Once Darius was on his knees, cock in hand, Jasmine gasped in surprise and pleasure as he slowly, gently eased into her. "Breathe," he commanded.

She nodded, glazed eyes fixed on Simon. He didn't dare move, despite his body urging him to, wanting to give her time to adjust to both of them being inside her. Behind her, Darius's face was a mask of controlled concentration, beads of sweat popping up along his brow as he fought for his own control. "How are you doing?" he asked, voice strained.

Jasmine nodded again. "Keep going."

Eyes squeezed shut, Darius eased himself fully inside her. Jasmine's breath came fast as she experimentally slid her body up, crying out when she fell onto their shafts. "Oh, God," she bit out.

"You feel so good," Darius grunted, withdrawing himself and thrusting again.

The feeling of both of them so close to him, their heat,

the intimacy of being able to look both in the eye beneath them, had Simon moving again. "She does," he said. He wouldn't last long now, but he was too far gone to care as he thrust into her.

Darius's mouth fastened on her neck as he did the same. Simon could tell he was already close too.

Jasmine came first, body clenching around Simon's as she nearly screamed her release. He didn't stop, needing to find his own. His gaze latched on to Darius's as he felt the first wave of orgasm wash over him. Darius looked at him helplessly, and Simon knew he was about to come too.

Jasmine collapsed against Simon as he and Darius came, her mouth kissing his in a clash of tongues and teeth. Hands gripping her hips through the pink fabric, Darius grunted, "I love you," with a final thrust into her.

Simon's heart soared. He didn't have the strength yet to speak the words as he spent inside Jasmine with a groan.

Simon wasn't sure how much time had passed when they pulled out of her to lie together on the bed in a tangle of bare limbs. Jasmine was snuggled between them, breath coming hard. "Did you mean it?" she asked.

"Oh, fuck, yes. I adore both of you," Darius replied. He ran a hand through his short, dark hair. "I love you both more than anything."

Simon had never heard those words before, hadn't known how much he'd wanted to hear them until now, even though he'd felt the same. "I love you both, too," he said.

Jasmine didn't reply, which didn't bother him. They had time enough to hear those words, and Simon wasn't sure if it was normal to declare love while climaxing, not that he had a great deal to compare it to.

She was with them now, sharing their lives. That was enough.

CHAPTER FIFTEEN

Jasmine's eyes fluttered open. To her left was Simon, wedged between her and Darius, both of them still deep in sleep. A bolt of heat coursed through her as the memories of the night before came flooding back.

She would *never* tire of waking up next to them.

Crumpled in a heap on the floor was her pink dress. She'd had to improvise it without a pattern and without other garments to work off of; she'd read about such a dress in a book long ago and had always daydreamed about creating one. She wasn't sure if she should be thrilled at Simon's and Darius's reactions at seeing her in it, or irritated with herself for not finding somewhere to drape it after they took baths last night. Both, she decided. She hoped the dress was salvageable.

Taking care not to disturb them, she crept out of bed. Her muscles protested, some in places where she didn't know she had muscles, another reminder of the night before. She couldn't keep a smile from her face despite the discomfort. She stretched her arms and back, then glanced behind her at the makeshift bed they'd been using. They really needed a proper one, big enough for the three of them.

I bet they never thought they'd need a bed big enough for three. Not a group of people who had once slept plugged into electric pods, standing up.

And they'd told her they *loved* her. She'd never heard those words from a partner, never expected to. When she remembered them saying that, she felt weak-kneed in a way that had nothing to do with their lousy bed. Her brain had been too scrambled to say the words back. She'd have to wait until they were all awake to tell them.

Picking up her discarded dress, she draped it over her arm. She tiptoed up the stairs, cringing at the boards creaking beneath her. On the wall, old holos and drawings from the Millmans, the people who had lived here before, beamed at her, a reminder of a life that no longer existed. Some of her good mood evaporated, replaced by sadness and regret. She hadn't known them well, since they'd passed away when she was young.

Jasmine washed up and dressed. When she returned downstairs, she found Simon and Darius already stirring. "Did I wake you? I tried to be quiet."

"We're cyborgs. Enhanced hearing goes with the territory," Simon replied.

"Why are you up so early?" Darius grumbled.

"I couldn't sleep anymore."

"There are things we can do in bed other than sleep, you know," he pointed out.

The tips of Simon's ears turned pink. Jasmine was sure hers were doing the same. "You two wore me out last night," she said.

"Ugh, fine. Some other time, then."

Any retort she might have offered was forgotten when their expressions suddenly shifted, faces going slack, eyes widening. The memory of Rhys's collapse came flooding back, and for half a second, she thought she might fall over herself. Just as quickly, their faces returned to normal. "We have to get up too," Darius said.

"Would you mind telling me what the fuck just happened?"

"Of course." Simon was already out of bed, moving so quickly, he was nearly a blur as he gathered his clothes from the floor. "The comms tower just got its first interstellar message."

Jasmine's relief at knowing her boyfriends weren't about to keel over and require emergency brain surgery quickly evaporated as Simon's words sank in. "What?"

"Rhys just told us over our shared link that it arrived this morning," Simon said, tugging on his trousers.

"Didn't even know he had that kind of range," Darius muttered. He picked up the tunic Jasmine made, grinned, and slipped it over his head.

"Oh, my God. Just tell me about the message!" Jasmine's voice had an uncharacteristic edge of hysteria to it. "Is it another cyborg group? Are we being invaded? We don't even have weapons!"

"It's nothing like that," Darius said, exchanging a look with Simon that she couldn't read.

"Oh, no. Do *not* start doing that! We're a team, remember?"

"Yeah, we definitely teamed up on you last night," Darius cracked. Simon set his head in his hands.

"Oh, my God, this is not the time!"

"Jasmine," Simon said, voice quiet and reassuring. He wrapped his arm around her. "Rhys doesn't think it's that serious yet. It, uh." He looked at Darius, who held up his hands and shrugged. "There's a delegation from an alien species on their way here now."

Jasmine's heart thundered against her ribs so hard that she was sure they must be able to hear it. "I don't know what to say," she said weakly, grateful to have Simon's arms holding her upright. "Why are they coming here?"

Darius replied, his tone more serious than she'd ever heard him before. "Well, it seems our previous clones stole their spaceship."

———

SHE WOULD *NOT* BE GOADED into staying home. As she did when their ship took off for the waystation, Jasmine followed Simon and Darius out of the house—*their* house, she reminded herself—as they strode to the comms tower. She had to jog to keep up with them and would have scolded them for it had she not been out of breath.

This is bullshit. What was the point of her holing up in the house, as they'd all but decreed? New Eden's population was next to nothing. She had no means to defend herself if the aliens got violent, and if they did, it was only a matter of time before they descended on the houses. If she was going to die today, she wanted to be with Simon and Darius when she did. Goddamn it, she still hadn't told them she loved them.

And Hannah. She had no doubt Hannah would be at the comms tower at Rhys's side. Come to think of it, Rhys would never command Hannah to stay home during an event like this.

She paused on the path to catch her breath. Simon and Darius continued on for a few more meters, then stopped and turned around. "Are you going to wait for me?" she asked.

They walked back the short distance. "I wish you'd stayed home," Simon said urgently.

"The whole settlement will be there," Jasmine pointed out. She could already see curious people wandering from their homes in her old neighborhood, heading for the tower. "Do you notice that no one is screaming blue murder? Maybe whoever these people are aren't here to punish you for stealing their ship."

"Technically," Darius began, but Jasmine cut him off.

"I know that *technically* you didn't do it," she said. "Didn't Rhys say if they were pissed off or not? Both of you were in such a rush to leave, you didn't tell me."

They exchanged glances. At least they weren't communicating telepathically, leaving her out of the conversation. She could tell when they did that, how their eyes went almost blank, like that part of their bodies had been shut off somehow. It was unnerving to watch. "He didn't say," Simon finally replied.

"So, wouldn't it make sense that maybe they aren't angry and just want their ship back? Wouldn't Rhys have told you if they were coming in with weapons hot?"

"How do you know about hot weapons?" Darius asked.

"Well, I've had sex with two of them," she replied pointedly.

Simon actually guffawed at the remark. Darius struggled to keep a straight face. She hoped she hadn't just doomed New Eden to an alien invasion by distracting them this way. "I read a lot before the earthquake, remember?" She thought about the pile of books she'd brought back from the waystation, guilt trickling through her. She'd hardly picked them up since then.

"Good point," Simon said. "And so is yours about Rhys telling us if they were armed."

"Unless they have tech that disguises it," Darius said. "Which is why we should hustle to the comms tower now." He sighed. "Which one of us will give her a ride there?"

Jasmine sighed, a little more dramatically than necessary. "You know you're just opening yourself up to another smartass joke."

"Hop on," Simon instructed. He bent down a little, and Jasmine obediently climbed on his back, like a picture of an animal from the old world. Koalas, maybe? No, opossums.

Then he and Darius took off with remarkable speed. She tried not to shriek as Simon bolted over the path so quickly that her vision blurred. She held on with all her strength, sure she would slide off him if she relaxed her grip even a little.

They stopped at the comms tower without so much as a gasp from the exertion. Jasmine crawled off Simon's back on shaking legs, letting both of them hold her up for a second as she regained her bearings. "Thank you," she murmured.

It didn't escape her notice that a few people looked at the three of them with raised eyebrows, but no one commented. Any worries she might have had about what others thought evaporated when she saw Hannah. They made a beeline for each other. "What's happening with the aliens?" Jasmine asked.

"We received a transmission early this morning from a group calling themselves the Si'laar." Hannah made a face. "I don't think I'm pronouncing it correctly. Anyway, they said they tracked down the cyborgs' spaceship and wanted to talk about it."

"That's it? Did anyone actually speak to them?" Come

to think of it, Jasmine hadn't wandered into the tower since it had been restored. She was afraid that if she breathed on something, she would break it.

"No, they sent a message and said they would be here at 08:00 hours, New Eden time."

Jasmine searched Hannah's face, looking for traces of panic. "You seem awfully calm about this."

She gave a half-hearted shrug. "I'm not, but Rhys isn't freaking out over it, so I won't, either."

"Rhys doesn't freak out over anything." She nearly quipped that he seemed to have had any nervous traits programmed out of him, but knew she probably wouldn't take that well. Not so soon after his emergency brain surgery.

"True, but I know he would tell me if he thought we were in grave danger. He'd tell everyone."

"Where is he, anyway?"

"Watching comms for their arrival. They sent a flight plan, too, and asked for the best place to land their ship."

"Are you sure it's safe for everyone to be here if a ship is going to come down soon?" Jasmine looked at the crowd. The comms tower was about twenty meters from the launchpad, still under restoration. A few cyborgs were piling it with bricks and materials brought back from the last trip to the waystation, including Simon and Darius. They moved with the same inhuman speed they had on the run to the tower.

Hannah sighed. "I have no idea."

The cyborgs working on the launchpad suddenly froze, then nodded at unspoken words and retreated to the tower. "What's happening?" she asked when Simon and Darius met her.

"The alien ship is breaking atmosphere. It'll be landing in a few minutes," Simon replied.

"Do we just sit here and wait to be incinerated?" The grumble behind them was familiar.

Hannah closed her eyes, as if to keep herself from whirling around to clock the speaker in the jaw.

Jasmine turned around instead. "Hey, Ollie."

Her neighbor had a furrow between his brows. At least he wasn't shouting or demanding everyone pick up sticks or knives. "Why is everyone so calm?" he demanded.

"I asked Hannah that already. If she and Rhys say we won't be blown to bits by whoever these people are, I believe them." She hoped she'd put enough conviction into her voice. More than that, she hoped she wasn't wrong about this. Her heart suddenly picked up its tempo as she realized that she was about to meet aliens for the first time. Second time, she reminded herself, thinking of the Dilorans at the waystation. She hoped whoever they were, they were as friendly as the Dilorans had been.

She thought of the black spaceship resting in the field outside the settlement. The *stolen* black spaceship. Her curiosity faded, and she thought she might be sick.

"I've had a good run," Ollie said wistfully. He sounded as if he expected to be the first to die.

A speck appeared in the sky, parting the thin white clouds. It slowly expanded until a flat, oval shape appeared, not unlike the cyborgs' ship. Tears sprang to her eyes, and she gripped Simon's and Darius's hands. They immediately wrapped their arms around her, and she breathed in their scents. "I love you," she said. "Both of you." She felt a watery smile spread across her face. "I wish I'd picked a better time to tell you."

"There's never a bad time to say that. We love you too," Darius murmured in her ear, his breath ruffling her hair. "Simon, if we're about to die—I should tell you I've loved you since I crawled out of that cloning tank."

Simon raised his free hand to trace a line along Darius's jaw. "I love you too. Both of you."

Behind them, someone coughed. Jasmine couldn't tell who it was.

A rumbling noise filled the air, and the wind picked up. Jasmine squeezed Simon's and Darius's hands, tried to let the feel of them relax her. It didn't work. She shot a look at Hannah, now held in Rhys's arms, her eyes wide as a sleek black ship descended to the launchpad. It was a much smaller version of the cyborgs' ship, but otherwise identical.

Silence descended over the crowd, with no one sure what to do next. Or maybe Rhys already had a plan.

He and Hannah untangled themselves and, hand in hand, walked to the ship, stopping about ten meters away from it. The ship's exterior door opened, its rampway extending to the ground. A tall, slender figure wearing a pale yellow robe appeared, a hood obscuring their features, then glided down the ramp. Jasmine blinked a couple of times, not believing her eyes. She finally spotted a pair of feet peeking out from the robe's hem as the figure walked toward Hannah and Rhys.

The figure stopped in its tracks a couple of meters from them and bowed, pale hands clasped together. Hannah and Rhys did likewise.

Hannah looked over her shoulder at Jasmine. "You can come over," she called.

Jasmine looked on either side of her. Simon and Darius gave each other the barest of nods, then, with their arms still around her, approached the alien.

Her fear gave way to curiosity as she took in the visitor. They towered over everyone, nearly glowing in the sunlight. Jasmine still couldn't see their face. Did the Si'laar have faces, the way humans and Dilorans did?

"This is Korjek," Rhys said, voice steady. "Korjek, these are our people. New Edeners and cybernetically enhanced clones."

"Hello. Thank you for hosting us," Korjek said from beneath the hood. The voice sounded raspy, reminding her of when she listened to the words her translator fed her aboard the waystation, but other than that, Jasmine couldn't tell anything from the tone.

"We thought it rude to refuse you, given we have your property," Rhys replied stiffly.

Jasmine held her breath, waiting to hear Korjek's reply. She thought the entire settlement had to be doing the same.

"There is time enough to discuss the theft," they finally said. There was an odd, strangely electric clicking noise through the words. "It has been so long since your kind helped themselves to our tech that we've long learned to live without it. Is there a suitable space for us to speak? My people are waiting aboard the ship. We cannot discuss this under the heat of your suns."

The only place big enough to hold everyone was the amphitheater, and Korjek had already said the outdoors was inappropriate. "What about the barn?" Jasmine blurted.

Hannah tilted her head to the side. "It smells like animals."

"It's the only place with a roof big enough for everyone to gather," Jasmine said. She hoped she hadn't just suggested the perfect spot for the Si'laar to murder everyone at the same time.

Korjek's head bobbed. "It is an enclosed building, yes?"

"Yeah, it's enclosed with cows." Hannah sighed and turned to Rhys. "What do you think?"

"I think Jasmine is correct. If everyone wishes to attend this summit, the barn is the only place large enough."

"Okay, then." Hannah raised her voice. "Everyone, if you want to go to this meeting . . ."

"We heard," said Ollie, already stomping in the barn's direction.

Hannah rolled her eyes. "Let's go."

CHAPTER SIXTEEN

THE MAIN AREA of the barn was filled with small tanks holding cloned chicken and bovine embryos. Newly repaired stalls held the calves and foals, occasional moos coming from them. New Eden's surviving chickens clucked quietly among themselves, pecking at the dirt floor. There were boxes of harvested vegetables, grown quickly with the cyborgs' tech, waiting to be processed.

But *was* it the cyborg's tech, after all? Jasmine sneaked a glance at Simon, who walked alongside her, his expression pensive. He was nervous, she could tell. When she looked at Darius, he flashed her a smile, but there were lines of tension bracketing his eyes and mouth that she knew hadn't come from their lack of sleep the night before.

Were they walking into a trap? Why did the Si'laar need to be out of the sun? Anxiety gripped her in an icy vise, despite the rising heat of the day.

In the center of the barn stood Hannah, who looked uncharacteristically befuddled at the situation. She threw up her hands in frustration. "Find a spot that seems the least uncomfortable," she called to the crowd.

Jasmine let go of Simon's and Darius's hands to meet her friend. "There's a chair in my sewing room," she said.

"That'll give us a little hospitality," Hannah grumbled.

Seeing Hannah irritated by the hosting duties and not terrified for her life set some of Jasmine's nervousness at ease. "You're really not worried about this?" she asked, voice low.

"Not in the way you might expect."

There went Jasmine's sense of relief. "You're not helping."

Hannah's dark eyes flashed, and Jasmine immediately regretted her words. "Excuse me?" Hannah snapped.

"I'm sorry, that didn't come out the way I wanted. I know you've done a lot for New Eden. You've done *every-thing* for New Eden. I'm scared shitless about the Si'laar, is all." Jasmine held her breath, waiting for Hannah's reaction.

After what felt like forever, Hannah sighed again. "It's okay. I know what you meant. I'm freaked out too, but I'm not scared of the Si'laar. If Rhys isn't too nervous, I won't be, either."

Any other conversation was halted when Korjek and Rhys strode into the center of the room. A few Si'laar trailed behind them, still wearing their hoods. Jasmine quickly hurried back to Darius and Simon and waited. Behind them, New Edeners and cyborgs alike were silent.

One of the Si'laar removed their hood, revealing golden-scaled skin and gills along their neck and pointed ears. The sight would have reminded Jasmine of the Dilo-ran, save for the long mane of snowy-white hair atop their head, and their height. All of the robed figures towered over the humanoids by at least a head. Pale eyes gazed out at the assembled crowd from beneath white lashes, their single white brow furrowed in concentration. Or maybe it was just the position it was supposed to be in. Of course, Jasmine couldn't read their facial expression or body language or identify its sex or gender.

The other Si'laar followed suit, revealing features nearly identical to the first one, save for different hair lengths. Were they clones too?

When the Si'laar spoke, their voice was gravelly, tinny. It reminded her of the crackle of static from the cyborgs' intraship comms aboard their vessel. *The Si'laar's vessel*, she reminded herself. Anxiety once again knotted itself in her stomach. "My name is Korjek," the Si'laar announced. "I wish to reassure you good people that we are not here to wreak vengeance upon you." Korjek paused. "I request confirmation that my translation is accurate."

"Thank God they're here in peace," muttered Ollie from behind Jasmine.

"Your translation is sufficient," Rhys said.

"One of our ships was absconded by a group of humanoid cyborgs seventy-one cycles ago," Korjek continued. "We traced it to this planet after our ship detected communications transmissions and recognized the . . ." They paused again. Jasmine guessed the translation device, wherever it was, was struggling to communicate. "Energy signatures. The transmissions marked the first outgoing communications from the ship since it was taken."

Rhys fidgeted, looking discombobulated for the first time in Jasmine's memory. "We know now that the cloning tech aboard the ship is Si'laarian," he shared. "It appears that our previous clones stole the ship for the tech to refine it for humanoid purposes. The sleeping pods are Si'laarian. They were adapted to accommodate us."

The barn was silent as the revelation sank in, save for the quiet clucking of a couple of chickens. Finally, Jasmine couldn't help but ask, "What about the beds?"

She felt herself flush as soon as the words left her mouth. Then she felt like an idiot for being embarrassed. She'd been on board the ship—she would know its features. Knowing that would have nothing to do with her relationship with Darius and Simon, which everyone knew about, anyway.

Korjek tilted their head at Jasmine's question. She guessed their translator was picking apart her question. "Many cycles ago, our people occasionally hosted delegations of humanoids. The human beds were a gesture of hospitality."

That made sense. Simon and Darius had told her they assumed as much, anyway. Before she could ask why they didn't deal with humanoids anymore, Korjek continued. "We are the last of our people and do not interact or interfere with other species. But our situation has changed. We are looking for a new planet."

"Just like us," Simon murmured, squeezing Jasmine's shoulder.

"This planet is not ideal. I fear that there are no ideal planets for the Si'laar left in the galaxy. We are nocturnal water-dwellers when not aboard our vessel," Korjek said. "We humbly ask that we be permitted to live in your waters by the light of day and on the land-mass when the suns have set. In return, we can share our technology with you. We confirm that your land-mass is not stable and your . . ." They paused, again searching or waiting for a word. "Infra . . . infrastructure is incomplete. The Si'laar can help with such matters."

"Let me get this straight," Darius said. "We stole your ship, and you're offering to *help* us?"

Korjek's pale eyes blinked. "You did not take a thing from us. Your predecessors did not abscond with our ship by violent means. We deduced that your people may have been desperate and could not ask for help."

Darius's eyes went blank, a telltale sign he was on the shared cybernetic link. When Jasmine glanced at Rhys, she saw the same look on his face. Rhys was probably telling Darius to shut the fuck up.

"Now, we are experiencing difficulties," Korjek continued. "We cannot thrive on an artificial environment aboard our ship indefinitely. May we live in your seas and landmass? We can construct our own domiciles."

"I'm not sure we're in a position to refuse," Hannah finally said after a long look at the crowd.

Jasmine held her breath, waiting to hear a commotion of arguments. None came. When she looked behind her at the crowd, she saw understanding on their faces that hadn't been present the night of the cyborgs' arrival. New Eden could not continue as it was without significant help.

"Should we have a meeting?" Hannah asked, when no arguments came back at her.

"God, no," called Ollie. "No more meetings. I hate meetings."

Did he, though? He was the first to complain about anything. Jasmine bit back a smile.

"I guess the Si'laar can stay, then," Hannah said.

There was a murmur of approval from the crowd. Simon pulled away a little, his voice booming. "Do you know anything about our origins?" he asked.

Korjek blinked. "We do not. Perhaps we can find out at a later time."

Did that mean they might know something about the original New Edener settlers? "What about our planet?" Jasmine asked. "Were our ancestors a bunch of pirates and smugglers?"

"I do not know what those are," Korjek replied.

"I'll try to explain it to you later." There was time enough to get into the details. Besides, there was still the northern expedition to consider. With a shock, Jasmine remembered that Rodelle would have no way of knowing what had happened, since she left for the trek. She was sure Rhys or someone would have told them if he'd been able to make contact with the group over their link.

"We can talk tonight, when the suns have set," Korjek said. "We are tired and wish to retreat to our ship for the daylight. Tonight, we can look for a suitable place in the seas." He made a low-pitched purring sound, and the other Si'laar pulled their hoods over their heads. Their language, Jasmine realized. Fascinating.

As the crowd trickled out of the barn, Jasmine tried to absorb what had just happened. New Eden had new residents, ones who not only didn't want to kill the cyborgs for their theft, but offered to help all of them. Un-fucking-believable.

She lingered behind everyone, deep in thought. She didn't realize almost everyone else had left until Simon draped an arm over her. "Is everything okay?" He and Darius wore concerned looks across their faces.

"Oh, yeah. I think everything is as good as it's going to get right now," Jasmine replied.

"Did you mean what you said earlier, when you thought we were all about to die?" Darius asked.

"About loving you? Of course, I meant it," she said, looking at each in turn. "I love both of you. I'm glad you didn't make me choose."

"That might've killed me," said Simon.

"Yeah, me too," Darius added. "Say it again."

"Simon, Darius—I love both of you to pieces."

Darius pressed a kiss to her lips that sent a bolt of heat straight through her. "We love you too."

Hand in hand, the three of them walked out of the barn, back into the brilliant sunshine. It took a few seconds for her vision to adjust, to see Hannah a few meters away, speaking to Rodelle. "Oh, my God!" Jasmine cried out and ran toward her.

Rodelle was deeply tanned after days of walking in the sun. Streaks of dirt marred her clothes and skin, and she had a wide-eyed look of wonder on her face that hadn't been there before. She looked almost happy for the first time Jasmine could remember. "Did you see the Si'laar?" Jasmine asked excitedly.

"No. What's that? The other ship in the field?" Before waiting for a reply, Rodelle forged on, words coming out in a rush. "What did I miss?" Without waiting for an answer, she blurted, "There's so much I have to tell you!"

Jasmine and Hannah exchanged a look. Hannah looked just as mystified—and excited—as Rodelle did. "Did you find answers in the north?" Jasmine asked, heart pounding.

"Oh, my God," Rodelle said. "You have no idea."

ABOUT THE AUTHOR

Jessica Marting is a sci-fi and paranormal romance author, art enthusiast (not quite an artist, despite all that time in art school), an avid reader, and makeup collector. She lives in Toronto.

Sign up for her newsletter at jessicamarting.com/newsletter for pre-order alerts, sales, freebies, and more.

Magic & Mechanicals

Wolf's Lady

Sea Change

Bound in Blood

Dragon's Keep

Spellbound

The Searchers

Blood Ties

Blood Moon

Blood Virtue

Zone Cyborgs

Haven

Paradise

Oasis

Safe Harbor

Sanctuary

Refuge

The Commons

Supernova

Celestial Chaos

Standalone Novels & Novellas

Spindle's End

Trade Secrets

Neon Vice

Dead Ringer

Rapture

Escape From Europa 10

Castaways

Demon's Favor

Her Purrfect Match